"What is going on, Evan?" Natalie asked, this time appearing more frantic than she had before.

"I don't want you to get upset." His words sounded out of place even to his own ears.

"I'm well past upset. What in the hell is going on?" Natalie seemed absolutely terrified—the one thing he had wanted to avoid.

"Don't worry. Everything will be fine." He knew she could hear the lies, regardless of the words he had chosen to try to assuage her terror.

She moved beside him and stepped to the window, but he pushed her back. Her eyes and mouth opened wide, as though he had struck her instead of attempted to protect her.

"I'm sorry, I didn't mean—"

"What in the actual hell—"

"There is another bomb." He spit the words like they themselves were a ticking time bomb.

Acknowledgments

Thank you to my fantastic team at Harlequin. This year has been one unlike any other, and yet they have continued doing their jobs to the best of their abilities and kept making authors and readers their first priorities—even at the cost of their own sanity (or so I assume).

I will always be honored to be a part of such an incredible group of individuals.

A JUDGE'S SECRETS

DANICA WINTERS

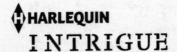

HARLEQUIN

INTRIGUE

To all those who have stepped into the flames and
kept moving forward.

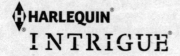

HARLEQUIN®
INTRIGUE®

Recycling programs
for this product may
not exist in your area.

ISBN-13: 978-1-335-55525-0

A Judge's Secrets

Copyright © 2021 by Danica Winters

This edition published by arrangement with Harlequin Books S.A.

For questions and comments about the quality of this book,
please contact us at CustomerService@Harlequin.com.

Harlequin Enterprises ULC
22 Adelaide St. West, 40th Floor
Toronto, Ontario M5H 4E3, Canada
www.Harlequin.com

Printed in U.S.A.

Danica Winters is a multiple-award-winning, bestselling author who writes books that grip readers with their ability to drive emotion through suspense and occasionally a touch of magic. When she's not working, she can be found in the wilds of Montana, testing her patience while she tries to hone her skills at various crafts—quilting, pottery and painting are not her areas of expertise. She believes the cup is neither half-full nor half-empty, but it better be filled with wine. Visit her website at danicawinters.net.

Books by Danica Winters

Harlequin Intrigue

STEALTH: Shadow Team

A Loaded Question
Rescue Mission: Secret Child
A Judge's Secrets

Stealth

Hidden Truth
In His Sights
Her Assassin For Hire
Protective Operation

Mystery Christmas

Ms. Calculation
Mr. Serious
Mr. Taken
Ms. Demeanor

Smoke and Ashes
Dust Up with the Detective
Wild Montana

Visit the Author Profile page at Harlequin.com.

CAST OF CHARACTERS

Natalie DeSalvo—The youngest woman to be a Montana district court judge in the state's history. She is a heroine of the people who has built herself on a foundation of power, control and a code of ethics that is almost as strong as the woman to which they belong.

Evan Spade—A personal guard employed by STEALTH's Shadow Team. Evan is a man who prides himself on being the best, but not even he can always keep evil at bay.

Mary Rencher and Sophia Sanders—A couple going through a contemptuous divorce, one which may or may not be filled with so much hate and nefarious dealings that it spills over into attacks on a judge.

Judge Hanes—Natalie's mentor and friend, a judge who has a collection of achievements, accolades and, unfortunately, secrets.

Sven Hanes—Judge Hanes's son, an employee of the city fire department thanks to help from his father's political pull.

Judy Becker—Natalie's adoptive mother and a woman whose primary goal is to make sure Natalie is safe, well-fed, and always feeling protected and loved.

Becky Jenner—Sven Hanes's girlfriend, who is as book smart as she is naive in love.

STEALTH—A private military contracting group that oversees several divisions, including the Shadow Team and the Spade siblings.

Rockwood—A crime syndicate whose leaders and associates are constantly at odds with the Shadow Team and their objectives.

Chapter One

Secrets had a way of feasting on a person's soul. Their appetite was voracious, parasitic in their inability to stop consuming until there was nothing left of their host but an empty shell. Judge Natalie DeSalvo had witnessed this parasitic invasion time and time again, and would continue to do so as long as people walked the earth.

This week had been especially brutal for Natalie; just that morning she'd had a case centered around human trafficking. One of the kidnapper's victims had been subpoenaed and forced to testify. When the woman had slipped into the courtroom, she had held her trembling hands together in front of her, and her eyes had never left the floor. Sweat beaded at her hairline and her face had been a sickly white. No doubt the victim feared for her life.

Natalie had asked the woman to look at her on the stand and had gazed directly into dark, nearly black eyes. In those seconds it was as if the woman's penetrating stare had acted as a vacuum, pulling every shred of empathy and pity from Natalie until it threatened to ooze out onto her notes and smudge the ink.

Her entire body had hurt for the woman as she had told her story of being taken to the streets of Las Vegas and sold. The secrets poured from her, faster and faster, as the lawyers pressed her, until finally, she no longer stared down at the floor. Soon, some of the life that had seemed stripped from her began to return, filling her until she changed from empty automaton to flesh-and-blood accuser. Her voice became stronger, and then—when she looked at her kidnapper—the world shifted.

The woman came back to life.

It was those moments of self-acceptance and that break from secrecy that made Natalie love her job. There were only a handful of moments that made her feel like she was doing what she had been destined to do. The rest of the time she felt as if she was just a cog in the wheel of the criminal defense system, a system she found to be broken as much as she felt it worked.

By the end of the trial, and after hearing all of the victims' testimonies about the atrocious things the man had done to them and their lives, she had sentenced the man to prison where he would serve twenty years, without the ability to seek parole. It was the maximum allowed for his crimes.

The sad truth was that, even if the trafficker spent the rest of his life behind bars, he could still get to this woman—even make sure she was killed if the mood struck him. Even doing everything Natalie could, the power she wielded as a judge wasn't enough to promise anyone any real safety.

It was no wonder that she was often hard-pressed for a good night's sleep.

Thankfully, the other district court judge, Steven Hanes, had been tremendously generous with his time and mentorship. Tonight she would need his ear and support more than ever.

She sighed as she packed up her things after the last trial of the day—one where a drunk driver had managed to get a jury of twelve to ignore his blood alcohol content and find him not guilty. That kind of thing was common. Often, there was someone on the jury who had gotten a DUI, or knew somebody who had, and comprehended exactly what kind of long-lasting ramifications came with a guilty verdict.

The man on trial had definitely played the pity card, talking about how he had been out of work and had just been trying to get out a series of résumés and applications when he'd been asked to have a drink with a potential employer. It was hard to know if the man was telling the truth or lying, but it was clear, based on his threadbare and too-small suit jacket, that he was down on his luck.

Little did the jury know, but the man had eight previous DUIs and this was nothing more than his best attempt to take advantage of the good nature of the people on the jury who only wanted the best for him.

He had walked away with the harshest consequence she could hand down—a warning not to repeat his mistakes.

Yes, this was one of the days she hated her job and the way that criminals so often knew exactly how to take advantage of others and the system.

She sighed and picked up her briefcase, slipping the strap over her shoulder, and the bailiff followed her out of the empty courtroom. She bid him goodbye with a nod and a small wave. Before she made her way from the courthouse, she stopped by Judge Hanes's chambers. He'd had a DUI on his docket, as well, and he tended to take these kinds of trials harder than she did. His first wife had died as a result of a drunk driver when she was struck in the middle of the day while trying to cross a street. The accident had left him a single father of a rowdy boy who had become an even rowdier man.

Judge Hanes was at his desk when she stuck her head in. "Heard you had a heck of a trial. You doing okay?"

He sighed and reclined in his leather wing-back chair, which sat behind his mahogany desk. "That was a tough day."

She smiled but felt a tiredness in her eyes that she couldn't blink away. "I'm sure you did what you could."

He waved her inside. "Why don't you come in, sit down? Or do you have somewhere to be?"

She loved hanging out with the age-wizened judge, and truth be told, she looked forward to their evening chats. Usually, he was like her, rushing about and needing to be somewhere, so it was a treat to receive the invite from the man she looked to as a father figure.

Besides, where did she have to be? Her house was empty and there was no one waiting for her at home. There hadn't been in four years, ever since she had kicked her ex-boyfriend to the curb. Since then, she had poured herself into her work and became the youngest female district court judge in Montana's history—some days, like this one, she wondered which had been harder, breaking up or being young and in power.

She walked into the office, clicking the door shut behind her.

"How did your case go this morning?" he asked, motioning to the chair across from his desk as he got up and went to the concealed side bar that was tucked away in the corner of his library beneath several shelves of law books. His lips were drawn into a tight line, and the creases in his brows were the deepest she had ever seen them. "Want a scotch?"

"Sure." She wasn't much of a drinker and she definitely wasn't a scotch drinker, but she always made the exception for Hanes. "I'm surprised that the man's lawyer didn't ask for a change of judge. If I'd been the lawyer on that case, it would have been the first thing I would have done. He couldn't have assumed a female judge would remain impartial in a case of trafficking women."

Judge Hanes scoffed. "You know public defenders. Most are so overwhelmed that they don't have time to tie their shoes let alone do the legwork required in high-intensity, emotionally riveting cases."

He opened a bottle of water and filled her tumbler halfway and then added a dot of scotch as though he was aware she was only going along with this for his benefit. He handed her the glass and then filled his own, the mixture more to his taste. As he sat down in his chair, he let out a long exhale.

She had seen him after many of these kinds of trials, but tonight he seemed more road worn than normal. "What's wrong?"

He chuffed. "That easy to tell?"

"I know you're a poker player, but tonight I would advise against hitting the tables," she said, hoping to lighten him up. "You want to tell me what's on your mind? I don't know how much help I'll be, but I'm willing to listen."

He took a long drink, nearly emptying his glass. This was unlike him. He wasn't a man about getting drunk; he was a man about making a statement. Whatever was on his mind must have been eating him up inside, making her wonder if this was less about the trial and more about whatever was happening in his personal life.

He cleared his throat. "I've always appreciated that about you. You're good people, Judge DeSalvo. It is all too easy to fall into the darkness that comes with our position."

Yep, he definitely wasn't being himself. He normally used her first name when they were in private…why the sudden shift to her professional moniker? What was the significance?

"What's on your mind?" she pressed.

He closed his eyes and sighed as if he was trying to decide whether or not he really wanted to open up to her, and it made her feel for him. Finally, he looked at her and there was a pain in his features she had never noticed before. "I'm trying to clean up some trouble. And because of it, now someone wants me dead." He took a drink. "I'm used to this kind of thing, but…"

She sat in shocked silence, waiting for him to continue and not wanting to rush him even though she wanted to ask about the threat. She couldn't believe how calm he seemed. Yes, he was thrown off balance and worn, but not overly surprised.

Hanes opened up his top desk drawer and pulled out a photograph. "I'm having a hard time dealing with the fallout." He slid the picture across the desk.

Picking it up, she looked at the image. Hanes was standing at the top of the steps that led into the courthouse on the day she had been made district court judge. The picture had been on the front of the local paper the next day and was now framed in her office. There were several court clerks, the sheriff and the district attorney standing around them. Everything looked as it should except Hanes had been circled. His face was ex-ed out. A note in Sharpie had been scrawled on the bottom. It read: "Your death is coming. Soon. Turncoat."

She dropped the picture and it skidded out from her before lurching to a stop. "Did you report this to the police?" She looked back toward the door. "I could go and grab the bailiff. Maybe he hasn't left for the night yet."

He waved her off. "No. I don't want the police involved. I have a feeling that their digging into this would cause more harm than good."

Troubled by that answer, she ignored it for the time being. "Why did they call you a turncoat?"

He shrugged. "To the guilty, we're all turncoats."

"Have you told anyone else about this?"

"Just a couple people."

"What about your son, Sven?"

"Not yet. He doesn't need trouble. He's still trying to find his feet at the fire station, you know." He refused to meet her eye.

She didn't doubt Sven was still struggling, not for a second. It was well known the only reason Sven had gotten the job and wasn't in prison—thanks to his alleged drug possession and several assaults—was because of his father. "What do you think he would say?"

"Sven? He'd brush it off, probably say something about it having to do with one of my cases." He ran his hands over his face. "And he'd probably be right. You know how this world of ours works. There is always someone gunning for us."

She nodded, trying to come up with advice that would actually do some good. For now all she could think was that it was best if she gave him an opportunity to get things off his chest. Judges received threats from time to time, and most of them were empty blasts of anger meant to instill fear, but with no real follow-up. Hanes was a tough man and had enough security in place that he would remain safe. That wasn't to say someone couldn't get to him if they wanted him to be hurt, but they would definitely have to know what they were doing.

"Wait," she said, thoughtfully. "How did you get the picture?"

He emptied his glass before standing up, and this time just going for straight scotch instead of watering it down. "I found it on my desk this morning."

"On *your desk*?" She sat back like the object she had been leaning on was directly responsible for the death threat.

He chuckled, then took another long drink. "Yeah. That's the thing that is bothering me the most about the whole deal. I can handle the occasional threats, no biggie. Only the cleaning staff had access at night, but they have been through security checks and clearances."

"You don't think it was one of them, do you? Was anything else amiss?" Her mind whirled as she thought about her own chambers—she hadn't noticed anything out of place, but she hadn't been looking. Thankfully, there had been no picture on her desk and no obvious threat.

He shrugged, the action so foreign coming from this man that panic filled her. "Nothing appeared tampered with and my desk was locked when I came in this morning, but you and I both know that safety is nothing more than an illusion."

Actually, no…she hadn't felt that way, not until right now. She knew criminals could find ways around the toughest security, but there was still a barrier.

How could this have happened? How could he be saying these things? Her anxiety intensified, but she tried to keep it in check by reminding herself that Hanes was a strong man. "I'm sure you will be okay, this will be okay," she said, her voice high and awkward as she lied.

To see him scared, terrified her.

He gave a sardonic laugh. "Here is hoping. But I've made a few calls to help me remain alive."

"What do you mean?"

There was a knock on the office door. Hanes smiled, the first time she had seen him do so since she came in the room. Getting up, he made his way to the door and as he did, she smelled the smoky aroma of scotch coming from him, making her wonder if he had been drinking before she had come to his office.

Hanes opened the door. Standing there, immaculate in his black suit, was the best-looking man she had ever seen in real life. He had short blond hair that edged the right way into red and a matching well-kempt beard. His sunglasses were perched on his head, and if she had to guess, he was some kind of agent. Had Hanes called in a joint task force?

Her body willed her toward him, but she resisted the urge. She didn't need anything that good-looking in her life. Nope. No way. Not today. Not ever. Good-looking men had a heck of a way of coming into her life and leaving her with nothing more than a bladder infection and a required date with her battery-operated best friend.

This was one man she would make sure to steer clear of; she didn't need antibiotics.

He walked into the office, smiling as he looked to her. Her cheeks warmed and she looked away from his green eyes.

She needed to get out more if this was going to be her reaction to handsome men in the same room with her.

"Good evening," Judge Hanes said, motioning for the man to take the chair next to her as if deliberately trying to make her squirm. "Thank you for coming on such short notice, Mr. Spade." He picked up a pen beside his computer and clicked it open and closed, a nervous tic she'd witnessed often.

"Please call me Evan." He gave the judge a nod in greeting, but extended his hand to her.

"Pleasure," she said, shaking his hand with as little contact as she could make happen without appearing to be a germaphobe. Even though their hands barely touched, she could still make out the distinct charge of attraction pulsing from her. Hopefully, he hadn't felt it, too.

"Evan is going to be working security for me," Judge Hanes said, his voice cracking. He cleared his throat and ran his hand over his mouth, looking physically uncomfortable. He cleared his throat again. "He is with STEALTH, a military contracting group out of Missoula here and he comes highly recommended." He coughed, taking another drink of his scotch. "Nice. Man," he croaked.

"I'm glad to see you hired some extra security," she said, trying to ignore the judge's discomfort. She looked over at Evan, heat once again rising in her as she caught his gaze.

The judge glanced at Evan, and as he did, she noticed his nose appeared to be taking on a strange purple hue. He moved to speak, but a strangled gurgling noise lurched from his throat, replacing his words.

"Are you okay?" she asked, jumping to her feet but two steps behind Evan, who was already standing beside the judge and had his hand on his back.

He collapsed toward the floor, but Evan caught him and laid him down gently.

"Do you smell that?" Evan asked, looking to her.

She shook her head.

"Mustard," he said. "Cover your mouth and get back."

She wanted to listen, she did, but instead she stood there in shock, watching.

After taking a black zippered kit out of his chest pocket, Evan opened it and pulled out a syringe. He plunged it deep into the judge's chest and pushed down the depressor before extracting the needle.

The judge coughed, harder and harder with each passing second. A bloody spittle dotted his lips and he glanced back up at her with wide, terrified eyes. His body went rigid and he started convulsing. Between his attacks, her honorary father whispered the words she had never known could strike so much fear into her heart, "It's...too late."

Chapter Two

The freshly dead had a distinct smell, usually that of body gases and drying blood. He hated it. To him, it was the odor of life's greatest fears. Most people avoided the sources of such things, and yet, he rarely had the luxury.

Dealing with death came with the territory of working in surveillance and military contracting for STEALTH, and it was one of his least favorite aspects of his job. If he smelled death at this range, either he had done something very right or very, very wrong—and damn if he hadn't caught a whiff.

In this case, if the judge died, his death would be on Evan's hands—he had failed to protect and he had failed at his mission.

Damn it all to hell.

He watched as the EMS workers put the judge into the back of their wagon and turned on their sirens to head toward the hospital. Hopefully, he had acted in time, injecting the pyridostigmine and atropine straight into the judge's heart. Though he wasn't the medic for his STEALTH team, they had all been trained in how to deal with chemical nerve agents that didn't immediately kill.

Thankfully, the police had yet to be called. When Judge Hanes had hired him for protection, he had made it clear he was to keep everything private, and any sort of legal action would be taken by Hanes himself and none other. So far as the EMS had been told, the judge had come into contact with some sort of allergen and had an anaphylactic response—thus the atropine. The doctors could figure out what had really happened with a little lab work.

In the meantime Evan needed to figure out who would have done this to the judge and why. And his first inclination was to look at the woman who had been sitting in the judge's office when he'd walked in. From what the judge had told him, there were only a small handful of people who were allowed into his private sanctum, and those were on an invitation-only basis.

"What is your name? We didn't seem to make it that far," he said, turning to face the blonde.

She didn't seem to want to meet his gaze, which only made the hairs on the backs of his arms tingle that much more. She was definitely acting guilty of something.

"My name is Natalie. Umm… Natalie De-Salvo. I'm a district court judge. Steven was my mentor."

Had she added those unnecessary details, details he hadn't requested, in order to passively tell him that she wasn't someone who would have been behind this attack on the judge? Something like that, preemptive information, was often a tell of guilt. And she had used past tense when talking about her *mentor*—odd for a person who didn't know if he was dead. But then again, nothing was ever simple when it came to his line of work in surveillance and security. Maybe she was as nervous as he was about what had taken place.

"Ah," he said with a slight nod. "Nice to meet you, officially. I wish it had been under slightly different circumstances, but here we are." He gave a dry, dark laugh.

She didn't seem to appreciate his humor and her face puckered with distaste.

"I am sorry about your friend," he said, meaning it.

"Thank you." She stared in the direction the paramedics had been. "Do you think he's going to make it?"

Evan shrugged. "Depends. The meds I gave

him should completely go into effect in about another fifteen minutes. Until then, he is in the EMS's hands."

"Yeah. By the way, what did you give him?"

Funny enough, he wanted to ask her the same question.

"Something to keep his heart pumping and neutralize whatever chemicals he had come into contact with—hopefully."

She scowled at him. "You think it was a chemical attack?"

For a woman who was topping his current suspect's list, she was either completely oblivious or playing oblivious rather well. Either way, he was going to have to keep her close until he had his answers.

"He presented with the correct symptoms. But we are going to have to dig into things."

Her frown disappeared. "We?"

"I need to know if you are in danger, as well, or if you were just at the wrong place at the wrong time." He smiled, as if trying to make her feel more comfortable. "I noticed you guys had glasses of something. Were you drinking together?"

She guppied for a moment, her mouth opening and closing, looking as if she had lost her words. "I...we...we were drinking scotch. I didn't drink much of mine. Just a sip." She paused. "Am I..." The words fell like ashes from her fiery lips.

"If you didn't have a reaction yet, you should be fine. Are you feeling okay?" He watched her green eyes, a shade darker than his. She looked terrified.

And yet, he couldn't let himself believe she was innocent just because she was a beautiful damsel in distress—his weakness.

He took a step back as if being just a few inches farther from her physically could also distance him emotionally and mentally from the woman.

"I'm okay," she said, looking down at her body and running her hands over her curvy figure as if she was looking for a bullet hole.

He held back a smile at her reaction.

He took another step away.

"You look okay, but I think we should go back to the judge's office. Take a look around before anyone else gets a chance to go in there. Do you have access?"

She nodded, but her mouth was still opening and closing slowly like she was trying to recover the words that she had lost.

"You are okay. This will be okay," he said, equally concerned and on guard. "We just need to learn exactly what happened."

She nodded and started to walk back into

the courthouse. He followed behind her, trying not to notice the way her pencil skirt hugged her hips.

Scanning her card, she keyed in the code through a series of doors until they were finally back into the judge's chambers. He watched carefully and was sure that, if push came to shove, he could get himself back into this area if the need arose. In fact, he couldn't help but feel like the security in this area and the courthouse was woefully lacking. The place didn't even have metal detectors. Any geek off the street could walk in, strapped. It would only take a bailiff being slightly distracted and just about anyone could get killed here. Even something like a shooting—hard to pull off in a building like this—wasn't out of the question if the wrong person had the right incentive.

And as for the courtroom, he couldn't think of a more emotionally fraught environment. Here there was everything, good and bad, but copious amounts of the latter. Just look at himself—no one had blinked an eye when he strode through the building. Those who worked here had been acclimatized to the risk; that was perhaps what made danger even more of a possibility.

Complacency was death's knell, and today it sounded for Hanes.

The one thing he couldn't make clear sense of was the mechanism of death. There were many easy ways to kill a person, and yet, this attacker had chosen poison. Strange.

He had often heard that poison was the work of a woman, but having been in Iraq he could definitely say with 100 percent certainty that poisons and nerve agents were just as likely to come from a man in a war-torn country. Chemical nerve agents were one of the most effective and deadly weapons on the battlefield. A tiny bit of sarin released via unmanned aerial vehicles, and an entire town could be wiped out in a matter of hours.

And that was to say nothing about the fear that a little white phosphorous could drive into a soldier's heart. Weapons like those had often kept him up at night and were some of the reasons he was glad he was back working in the States—for now.

Yep, he liked his McDonalds and Americans' conversations about politics far more than just about anything that came with standing in the middle of a war zone. And yet, there was always one thing that drew him back into the fray—adventure.

There was nothing better than the feeling of being alive after a day spent just millimeters from death. That crap was addictive. It was like taking a straight shot of adrenaline each and every day. Being without it felt exactly like what he assumed drug addicts went through when they were trying to get clean.

This life, *his* life, was a drug, and damn if he couldn't ever get enough.

Natalie turned to face him as they entered the judge's office. "Here you go. What do you think we should be looking for? What are you thinking? How can I help?" In finding her words again, she seemed to want to say them all at the same time.

"Hard to say, but I'm sure I will know it when I see it." He didn't actually believe what he was trying to sell her, but he had to fake it until he made it.

One of the most common chemical nerve agents was sarin gas. But if their attacker had used that against the judge, how had he and Natalie not been affected?

He mulled over the thought as he walked around the spacious office, touching nothing. Everything seemed to have its place and was in immaculate order.

He kept his house and his apartment at the STEALTH compound just as clean. He was constantly picking up after his siblings' messes. A tiny smile took over his lips as he thought about his brothers and sisters and their dream team for STEALTH. Life had been amazing in bringing them all together and working for the same company. The past year had been fun, relying on one another and working as a well-oiled unit of people he knew without a doubt he could trust with anything—even things more valuable than his life.

Walking to the corner of the room, he noticed there was an open cabinet door beneath a number of shelves of books. Inside was a collection of what he recognized as expensive bottles of scotch. The judge had good taste. On the edge of the shelf was an opened bottle of water.

Sarin could be mixed effectively with any liquid. Was it possible that someone had drugged the water bottle, knowing how the judge took his scotch?

He didn't want to sniff the open container, but at the same time if there was any sarin in the water it was unlikely to give off much of an odor. He wafted his hand over the top, but all he detected was the mineral-rich scent of expensive bottled water.

Sarin, if in its impure form, could smell of either burned rubber or mustard. He'd caught a tinge of that when the judge had collapsed.

And yet, he reminded himself, he wasn't even sure if that was what they were dealing with here or not. There were a number of chemical nerve agents, many of which he probably hadn't even heard of yet.

Natalie tapped him on his shoulder.

"Hmm?" he asked, turning away from the side bar and glancing at her.

She looked afraid, her skin pale and a thin layer of sweat on her brow. "Steven had a tic." She pointed to the judge's desk.

"Okay," he said, the word coming out more like a question.

"When he was deep in thought, he always clicked his pen. Some days it drives me absolutely nuts." She pointed at a pen that rested beside his keyboard. "He clicked it when you walked in. Do you think someone could have delivered a nerve agent with that?"

Hell yes, they could have.

He nodded, trying to tamp down his excitement at a possible source. "Good idea." He pulled a Ziploc bag out of his back pocket and flipped it inside out over his hand. Moving to the desk, he picked up the pen and folded the bag around it, careful not to let the pen touch his fingers. As he zipped it closed, he caught the faint, distinct aroma of mustard again. He clicked the pen; at its tip was a ruptured rice-size capsule.

They had their suspect's weapon.

Chapter Three

He was watching her; Natalie could feel it. This security guard, this ridiculously good-looking man who probably had a variety pack of smoldering gazes at the ready, was staring at her. She hadn't blushed this much since she was in high school. What was wrong with her?

There were a million things she should have been concentrating on—making it to the end of the day would have been a great start—and instead here she was, twitterpated by Mr. Sexy Face.

She watched him carefully hold the bagged pen. He looked irritated. "Everything okay?" she asked.

"Huh? Yeah. Fine." His words rang false. "I think it would be best if we get out of here. If there has been a nerve agent deployed in here, we can still be in immediate danger."

"So you are now sure that was what happened? You don't think it could have been anything else?" she asked. She had been hoping against all hope that the attack had been something besides what he'd suggested.

He showed her the pen and its exploded tip. "This was definitely filled with sarin gas, or a close derivative of it. You are lucky to be alive." He took her by the arm and gently led her out of the office.

She felt the ache in her gut grow more intense. He had told her that she would have already been affected if she was to have been targeted by the attacker, but she didn't know this man from Adam. He could have been telling her anything just in an attempt to make her feel better.

If she didn't have anything to worry about, then why would he have been in a big rush to get her out of the office? Was he concealing critical information…or bad intentions?

At the realization, some of her insta-attraction diminished. Yes, more of that. She had to get this lust fest under control, and by thinking him a jerk, it would work like a charm. And she definitely didn't like that a man would just take her by the arm and lead her, but then again, he was trying to save her from being further exposed to a potentially lethal nerve agent. Yet, it still irked her.

Yes. She smiled at herself. More derision toward his behavior and she would be out of lust in no time.

"Is there anyone else working in this area right now?" he asked, looking around and then toward the ceiling as if he was searching for an overhead camera.

Yeah, right; we are closer to Flintstone tech than the Jetsons up in this place.

She glanced down at her watch. "The cleaning staff normally starts coming in an hour. They will be throughout the building for the rest of the night, but for now it is pretty quiet here."

"No cameras?" he asked.

This time his question made her wonder why he was so keen on knowing if there were potential witnesses nearby. "Why do you ask?" She stepped back from him. "The sheriff's department headquarters is just one floor up and we have deputies coming and going all the time. There are plenty of people around who'd catch a criminal in the act." It was as close to a threat as she could muster.

"I thought you said this place was pretty well deserted for the next hour or so?" he said, giving her a half-cocked smile that, if she hadn't been leery, would have been what her best friend Kristin called a panty-dropper.

She'd always loved Kristin, but in this moment she could have kicked her butt for making her want to smile when she was facing down a potentially dangerous man.

Actually, forget the *potentially.* Rather, he *was* dangerous—in so many ways.

"Look, I don't know if you're trying to freak me out or if you are trying to impress me, but it isn't working," she lied.

His smile widened and he looked at her like he was trying to figure her out. She liked it; in fact, she always liked surprising the people she was around. There was nothing worse than being predictable.

"You are a funny woman, you know that?" he said, doing a quick up and down of her body. Not so much to be crude, but enough to let her know that he was actively checking her out.

And there went her cheeks again. Before he could notice, she turned away and walked toward the employee exit and the parking lot.

"Where are you going?" he called, and she could hear his footfalls behind her as he rushed to catch up. "I think it's best if we stick together."

She stopped and huffed. Sticking together was the last thing she needed with this dude. "Look, you're not my boss. I've worked my whole life to get where I am and to no longer have to put up with men who think that they can push me around or tell me what to do," she seethed. "And strangely enough, the only man who remotely has any influence in my life is now lying on a gurney…after you were hired to protect him."

He went slack jawed. "What? Huh? Do you think… You are crazy if you think I had something to do with that attack."

"I didn't say you did, but you certainly jumped to your own defense. Something you wish to get off your chest?" She glared at him, looking for any signs of guilt.

"I… You…" He bristled, puffing up like some kind of porcupine.

"I'm not just some demure woman who you can lead around by the nose just because you know you're handsome…umm… I meant somewhat attractive." She felt stupid for letting her inside voice sneak past her filters and spill out of her lips.

He deflated, as if her backhanded compliment was the needle it took to bring him back down to normal size. He smiled that stupid, half-cocked smile she loved to hate. "You think I'm handsome?"

"Whoa there, Fabio, just because I said you were *somewhat attractive* doesn't mean that you can get off the hook for being a total—"

"Hunk?" he said, finishing her sentence with a laugh.

"Oh, heck no. I was going to go with pain in the ass," she said, throwing it back at him.

"And you're a ballbuster, so what a pair we could make."

"Wow, you didn't…" she said in forced outrage, but secretly her mind raced toward the picture of the wedding dress she had taped up in her bathroom when she'd been in high school—lace with full sleeves. Beside it had been a picture of Ruth Bader Ginsburg. She didn't regret her decision to myopically focus on her goal of becoming a judge, but there had been many sacrifices in her personal relationships.

He gave her that sexy half grin again.

"Seriously, Fabio, cool your jets or you are going to be on your own." She gave him a side eye, waiting to see if he'd try using working together as an excuse to find a way to sneak into her bed.

"Not being Fabio, I swear. You are a beautiful woman, that goes without saying, but I don't need to *cool my jets* because they weren't fired up. I don't fantasize about having sex with every hot woman I meet. I just want you close because I think it's very possible you could unwittingly know who planted that pen in the judge's office. You showed me exactly how much access you have to him."

Now she felt like the porcupine—on one hand he thought she was hot and on the other he didn't want her, and then he also seemed to think she was bordering on inept. "I... I have known Steve since I was a child growing up in Missoula. I have worked with him since I first started as a clerk. He took me under his wing and helped me figure out the steps I needed to take to get where I am today. He has always been like a father figure to me. So yes, we know a lot of the same people, but like all judges, he has a million enemies."

He looked her over like he was searching for some kind of hole in her story and she hated it. Was there a part of him that thought she had something to do with Hanes's poisoning? "It is the ones closest to us who can do us the most harm."

"If you think I had anything to do with this, you can stop right here and right now. I don't break laws. I enforce them." She could feel the burn of her words on her tongue; hopefully, he felt the heat, as well.

He nodded, but she could feel his gaze boring into her and it did nothing for her anger. "Good."

"In fact, as an officer of the court, I should

be talking to law enforcement right now, not a man who was hired to provide security and failed and whose vocabulary probably doesn't include the word *justice*."

He jerked as he looked up at her, hurt in his eyes. "I know you think you probably know me and know the people I work with, but you don't, Your Honor."

She had heard her title spoken by a thousand different people in as many times, but rarely had she heard it uttered with the level of derision in his voice.

Her anger oozed from her as she looked back up at his bearded face—no one dared to speak to her as he had.

There were gray flecks in his beard in and around his jawline that accentuated the lines around his mouth. She would bet his beard was soft, not the harsh, coarse kind that most men kept. For a split second, she imagined the texture against the tender skin of her inner thigh.

Look away, woman. She could almost hear her friend Kristin's voice talking to her.

She just needed to get laid, then whatever this craziness was that she was feeling could be stuffed back into the recesses of her stony heart and she could focus on the reality of the situation they were dealing with. Sexual tension never led to positive outcomes anywhere except for those brief moments of bliss between the sheets.

"Okay," she said, sighing as she looked at her car at the far end of the parking lot. "So we can both agree that neither of us would have done this to Steve even though we both *could* have?"

"Same page." Evan nodded. "And I apologize for losing my temper. I… You deserve a higher level of respect than how I just treated you. I'm sorry. As to talking to the law, let's keep in mind that the judge didn't want to go there, so if you can hold off on that, he'd probably appreciate it."

She considered his request and sighed. He was right. Justice Hanes had brought him in so he wouldn't have to get officers involved. She could honor that request, too, at least for a little while. She cocked a brow, shocked by his reversal and self-awareness. "Thank you. I've worked really hard to be where I am. There are always those around who wish to tear away at my foundation in order to build themselves up."

"I understand that," he said. "Which brings me to my next question—"

"No, I'm not single," she lied, teasing him.

He actually looked crestfallen for a moment. What kind of game were they playing?

She wished she could bring the words back. It was only her anger that had made her say them in the first place. In any other atmosphere and after any other day, she could have given this handsome, suit-clad man a run for his money in the bedroom department, but why did he have to saunter into her life today of all days?

"That's disappointing," he said. "But not exactly where I was going with my questioning. Rather, I was going to ask if you knew of anyone in particular who would have had a motive for wanting Judge Hanes dead."

"I'm sure he told you about the photo someone left on his desk? I would assume the attacker was behind the threat." She walked down the marble steps that led to the main floor of the courthouse; their footfalls echoed out and filled the empty halls.

"He did, but he only spoke to me briefly and at that time he didn't mention any possible suspects. Did he tell you who may have placed that in his office?"

"I told you everything I knew." She sounded just a touch surly and as she realized it, she noticed the heavy look on Evan's face. "Sorry," she said, hoping to make things slightly less tense between them. "I just mean that if he didn't tell you, then he sure as heck didn't tell me. Steve was a man who kept his thoughts and feelings pretty close to his chest about most things."

"So you can't think of anyone in particular? Someone who he had seen in the courtroom?" He opened the door leading out to the parking lot and held it for her until she passed by him. He smelled of expensive, fresh-scented cologne and she took it deep into her lungs.

She started to walk toward her car. "There are plenty of people who Judge Hanes had ruled against. Between those people and their families, I would say that would put about a quarter of the city's population on our possible suspects list."

It took a special breed to want to put themselves and their families at risk in order to cast judgments down in the name of justice, social mores and civil control. They all knew the risks that came with their calling. And it was partially this risk that kept her from seeking real relationships—she chose this life; she wouldn't impose it upon others.

"I was always proud of the rulings that Steve made," she continued. "There is none that I can think of that was unjustified. If anything, I think he was very careful to adhere to the letter of the law even when he was aware that the truth lay somewhere in the gray area. And he was good with the members of the public who served on his juries. He is a good man."

"If I had any lingering doubts about you trying to murder him, I think that little speech would have cleared you," Evan said with a laugh. "I bet he was glad to have you around if this is the kind of support you always gave him."

She laughed, waving him off. "Oh, we had our fair share of moments when we butted heads, but I knew my place, and he was like a father or brother to me, nothing more."

"And your husband?"

There was the heat again. "I was kidding about being with someone. No husband. No kids. No boyfriend. I don't even have a dog. So no, there is no one in my life who would have had anything against him."

Evan looked away from her, but as he did, she was pretty sure that she had finally spotted a bit of color moving into his cheeks. Yes, at least it wasn't her this time.

"As I'm sure the judge told you, his son Sven has had a lot of run-ins when it comes to the law."

Evan nodded. "He mentioned his son, and I'll look into him, but he made it sound like his son was at the bottom of our list. He seems to have gotten his life squared away. And he has no motive."

She clicked her car's key fob. As she hit the button there was a strange sound, a loud click instead of the slide she was accustomed to.

Before she could take another step, Evan had wrapped his arms around her and was pushing her to the ground. As he threw her down, there was a *whoomph*. The air of the shockwave pressed down on her. The heat of the blast scorched the skin of her back, and her polyester skirt was forming around, and melting into, the backs of her legs.

The bomb was deafening in the parking garage and her ears rang. There was the sensation of liquid in her ears. Blood, maybe?

There was the scent of burnt hair and it stung her nostrils.

Work. She had been at work. They had been walking. There was an explosion. Her car.

There was a side-view mirror burning on the ground to the left. Reaching up, she felt the stab of shards of glass across her cheek.

She struggled to get up, but there was a strange weight on her body. Her car. Had something landed on her? She couldn't make sense of exactly what was going on.

On top of her was Evan. He was staring at her and yelling something, but she couldn't hear him. Instead, she could only see his lips moving. All she could think about was the fact that someone, some stranger, wanted her dead.

Chapter Four

Thanks to all his working security, this was certainly not the first time he'd been asked to escort and guard a high-risk target, but it was the first time he had two attempted murders within such a close period. Not only that, but the methods were so innately different. It was one thing to be schooled in the art of chemical warfare and be proficient enough to sneak into a courthouse and into a judge's chambers without being noticed, but to have a suspect who was also more than capable in car bombs was unusual. In a terrible way, their perpetrator was incredibly skilled; that, or they weren't working alone.

This level of desire to kill was reminiscent of Evan's time in Beirut when it was at the height of civil unrest. If asked, he wouldn't even be sure that this wasn't worse. In Beirut he was constantly barraged by a variety of enemies—from Hezbollah to radical political leaders—

but the one thing they all had in common was that when they attacked, they didn't hide who they were or why they were doing it. They wanted the world to see they were strong, and they wouldn't shy away from striking down anyone who stood in their way.

This perpetrator wanted to hide in the shadows and fears created by their crimes. Whoever was trying to get her into their sights literally could have been standing behind them and they would have never known.

The one thing every country and culture had in common was that danger lurked everywhere.

Judge DeSalvo sat on the curb and looked at what had once been her Honda Accord. Its shell was still burning, and he could make out the shrieking wail of fire trucks and ambulances as they careened through the downtown streets toward them.

After assessing she was all right, he'd helped her up and away from the fiery vehicle, making sure her injuries were superficial, and she wasn't going into shock.

By now someone in dispatch had to be taking note about the many mishaps taking place at the courthouse. Next, snipers would be lining the roof and bearing down in a show of force that would hopefully prove to be unnecessary.

"Judge DeSalvo, are you okay?" he asked.

She simply nodded, staring out at her car, her gaze unwavering.

"Judge Hanes recommended we try to keep whatever happened under the radar. How do you think we should handle this?" He knew she would feel compelled to work with local authorities more than ever now.

Finally, she looked away from her car and up at him as he hovered over her. "I know he hired you for his protection, but he couldn't have possibly foreseen this level of violence. If he had, there's no way he would have asked you to keep this from law enforcement."

He nodded. There was only so much hiding and sweeping under the rug that could be done—especially when it came to such a public attack. "Whatever you choose to do here, know that as long as you're in someone's crosshairs, I'm going to be here to protect you. My team and I will do everything in our power to keep you safe and neutralize your enemy."

She ran her hands over her face, leaving behind little trails of fresh blood on her cheeks. "I've always prided myself on standing against vigilante justice. There's a reason we have laws and there's a reason that I am the one the general assembly elected to enforce them."

He should have known that this would be her response. Justice could be sought in other places besides the courtroom. Yet, he wasn't sure that now was the time to argue the value of striking an enemy down without the law ever being involved. If he tried, she would think that he was some kind of masochist, or sociopath.

Sometimes, his greatest ally was silence.

It was one of the things he loved the most about his world and his teams. They didn't require anything beyond knowing what their objectives were and what it would take to reach them. Once the mission was completed, they didn't expound upon their glories or celebrate the wins. The only time they even spoke about past missions was to correct major flaws in their future procedures.

The sounds of the sirens grew nearer and as they approached, the anxiety in his gut intensified. Many former contractors with military-style organizations became law enforcement officers, but that didn't mean he would get an easy ride when the LEOs rolled up on this scene.

Just because someone had the same mentality at one point in their life didn't mean they presently had the same goals. Law enforcement officers had to answer to a hierarchy and public opinion, whereas contractors had more freedom—so long as they didn't take advantage of it.

Being in the limelight was for suckers.

He wasn't a sucker. "Judge DeSalvo, I know you want to do the right thing here, but I think we need to get you to a safe location." He wrapped his arm around her shoulders, and surprisingly, she didn't pull away. She seemed so strong, physically and emotionally, and yet, she leaned into him like she yearned for his support.

She nodded, weakly.

He held open his hand and she took it, allowing him to help her stand. She still gripped her briefcase as if it connected her to her life before the explosion. "You don't need to sit out in the open and wait to take a bullet all in the name of doing the honorable thing."

She spit out a laugh, the sound in direct contrast to the serious scene around them. He was relieved to hear it, and happy he had been able to give her the ability. He walked with her, leading her toward his truck—the only place he knew that she would be guaranteed safety. As he helped her into the passenger seat, the first set of ambulances arrived.

Her hair was disheveled, the blood was starting to dry on her cheeks and there was gravel on her chest from where she had lain upon the pavement, but aside from that she appeared outwardly unscathed—emotionally was another matter, but no ambulance or medical professional would be able to whisk away the trauma she had just endured.

Traumatic events had different effects on each individual. He had seen more than one man vomit after mortar rounds had exploded in the cars next to them, while others shrugged off similar events like they were nothing more than a Tuesday at the office. Admittedly, the latter were seasoned. How they had been affected by the death and mayhem when they had first encountered it was something they would likely never talk about.

In those moments in which a person was forced to see who they were at a noncognitive, purely instinctual level, few impressed themselves. People who experienced traumatic events had to confront themselves on a primal level and often were disappointed with what they found.

Ugh. He pulled on his beard as he made his way around to the driver's side of his truck. *Maybe I'm feeling too much. I need to shut that shit down. Feelings got people killed.*

Whatever was going on inside him was something he could think about later; right now he needed to focus on his job. Bury that stuff; deal with it later.

He rolled his shoulders and climbed inside,

his game face on. "Are you in any physical pain?"

She looked up at him, a look of surprise on her face. Had she noticed that he wouldn't even use the word *feeling* in order to check on her? Or was it that she had picked up on the steel doors closing over his core?

"I'm fine."

"Let's grab one of the EMS workers and have them come over and check on you." Although she'd seemed to have only superficial injuries, he didn't want to take a chance.

She opened her mouth as if to speak, then clamped it shut and stared down toward the glovebox. They sat in silence for a long moment. He didn't press her. "I'm fine. Just... Let's go." She spoke slowly, like her words were fighting each other for air.

He hesitated, wondering if he should go against her, but he didn't say a word. Instead, he started the truck and pulled out of the parking lot. They passed by a firetruck as they exited.

There was nowhere either of them had to be, nowhere that he could think of to go and nowhere he could think of taking her. Yes, there were the easy options: her place, his private house, his apartment at STEALTH HQ, or even a motel where neither of them would be recognized and where she could be safe. All of them were reasonable options, but none of them felt exactly right.

He hadn't been prepared for this outcome—he'd gone in for a meeting and come out with two attempted murders.

There was a right response to this situation; he just had to find it and put his dick back in his pants.

His truck's blinker clicked, the monotone sound barely audible over the road noise as he drove toward the interstate. He pretended to have a plan as he got on I-90 and started rolling east, toward Butte. Butte…there was an option. He could hole her up in some small B&B until this mess rolled over.

He glanced up at his rearview, looking for any possible tails. There was a white sedan three cars back, which had been behind them for at least three blocks before they had hit the on-ramp. He took the next exit, but when the white car didn't follow, he got back on the interstate. He half expected the judge to ask him what he was doing and why, as she didn't seem like the kind of woman to sit idle while in a time of turmoil, but she sat with her hands folded in her lap.

Would she continue to surprise him? People rarely did.

Most people were woefully predictable. In

fact, there were a multitude of psychological studies that stated the brain of a listener normally could tell what a person speaking to them would say three words ahead of whatever was actually said. Remarkable science, but it only spoke to how unoriginal people could be. His thoughts moved to technology and big data. It was really no wonder that the internet and artificial intelligence had grown leaps and bounds, being one step ahead of the people actually using them. It was no secret that this accumulation of data, then mixed with the predictability of human nature, could be so dangerous.

STEALTH was deep into the world of black ops and tech warfare. So much so, that his boss, Zoey, was working on creating a new team just to handle the tech side of things. She had been doing a tremendous job, but unlike big data, she didn't have an automated system. She still required hands on a keyboard.

"Where are you right now?" the judge asked, pulling him from his thoughts as he drove down the highway.

He gave her a look of surprise. "What? What do you mean?"

"I mean, obviously you were thinking about something or someone right there. You going to tell me who she is?"

Oh, she is good.

She could try to elicit information from him all she wanted, but that didn't mean he would let her in. "You need to save your questions for the bench on that one, Your Honor."

She cocked an eyebrow, but she didn't continue her line of questioning.

After a long, quiet moment, he wished he had told her that she had been off the mark and that he hadn't been thinking about a woman— at least not a woman in the sense she assumed he was. There were no *women* in his life, not that way. He hadn't been with a *woman* in at least a year—not since his divorce.

Really, what did it matter what she knew or didn't know about his private life? All she needed to know was that he was there to help her and he would come between her and a bullet if needed. Anything beyond that was irrelevant. He was a damned professional, even if his heart wanted to make him become less than.

And yet, that gave him no right to be cold; he could be a decent human being to her and still have boundaries. "Sorry if I came off a little rude there. It's just, well, I'm not great with women. Or people, for that matter."

Some of the tension on her face diminished. "It's okay. I know how important it is to keep some secrets to oneself."

"Agreed, but I hope you accept my apology."

"Done. Now, are we going to go to the Canadian border?" she asked, laughing a tiny bit as she flipped down the visor and started to sweep away the crumbling dried blood on her face. "If we are, I probably need to run home and grab my passport."

He chuckled. "Are you telling me that you are good with just dropping everything and running away?"

"Well, given that no judge appears to be safe at the courthouse right now... I have to think I'd be better off just about anywhere other than there." She sent him a smile as she rubbed a smudge of dirt off her left cheek.

She must have been starting to feel better, as she had finally seemed to once again find her voice. Pulling her cell phone from her briefcase, she started to text someone.

"I'm sure I don't need to tell you this, but whoever is coming after you may very well be able to track that thing in your hands there." He motioned to her phone.

"I was just texting my secretary so he could take care of my upcoming trials and have them rescheduled or reassigned. He's also telling police I'll be in touch shortly since they obviously know of the car bomb, if not about Judge Hanes." She shot him a thin smile. "I'm putting myself at your mercy. You better be able to keep me safe. Can I assume I'm in good hands?"

Had she missed the part where he had been hired to protect Judge Hanes and yet Hanes had nearly died? If he was in her shoes, he would have told himself to get lost. He just had to fake it and make her feel like he was in complete control. A little "nothing to see here, folks," mixed with "I'll be back."

He chuckled at the thought.

"Are you laughing at me?" she asked, her smile growing.

"Hardly," he said. "I was just thinking about Arnold Schwarzenegger."

"Really? I ask if you can be trusted and you go full *Terminator* on me?" She shook her head, playfully. "You are such a dude. I should have guessed exactly what kind of moviegoer you were the moment you walked into Judge Hanes's office."

"Oh, hey now, what is that supposed to mean?" he countered. "Were you judging me?"

She laughed, the sound high and bright and in complete juxtaposition to the reality in which they had found themselves thrown. "That *is* my job."

She had a point. One that was completely in-arguable. And yet, that didn't keep his curiosity at bay. "And what exactly did you think of me when you first saw me?"

She gave him a sidelong look, like she was trying to decide whether or not she would tell him the truth or pass off some kind of altered version of it. "I thought you looked competent."

Competent. He was really secretly hoping for something more like hot or devilishly handsome, but he would take competent.

"Fine compliment, coming from a woman like you. You are certainly *competent* yourself."

She smiled and her eyes brightened. The simple action made her look ten years younger and for a moment he wondered exactly how old she was. If he had to guess, she was probably about thirty, but he would never say it aloud. If anything, she looked younger than he was. And she was far more beautiful than any female judge he had seen before. Not that he'd been around too many judges; it wasn't in his nature to find himself in a position that required him giving testimony.

"It's funny that you should say that about me," she said, sounding contemplative. "There are many voters who think that it was a mistake to put me into the position that I'm in."

"Why do you say that?" he asked, careful not to assume anything.

"First, I'm a woman. This is Montana. We

aren't known for being especially progressive. Though, I like to think that is changing." She nodded, a look of pride in her eyes. "Second, I'm the youngest woman ever to be seated as a district court judge."

So she was likely around thirty. He didn't know a ton about the demographics of political and judicial positions, but he could guess at that one. "You must be incredibly proud of all that you have accomplished in such a short time. Seriously, you are an amazing woman."

"I told you, I wouldn't have been able to do it all without Judge Hanes's mentorship. He has been an incredible advocate." She sounded nearly reverent about the man, which made him wonder exactly how far their friendship went, but he didn't dare to ask.

He liked her and if she admitted that she had something with the older, fatherly type judge he wasn't sure how it would color his opinion of her. But what did that say about him? Who was he to have an opinion on who she slept with? It wasn't even his business, though technically in this circumstance it did border on his "needing to know."

"Is he married?"

Her brows furrowed. Of course, she would know what he was thinking even though he thought he had done a pretty decent job at hedging on the question of their past without actually asking.

"No, I haven't seen him naked. No, he is not married. And no, there is no romantic attachments between us," she said, nearly snarling. "You know, it is exactly that kind of thinking that has stood in the way of a woman being in a position like I'm in now. Everyone just assumes that for a woman to get ahead she had to sleep her way to the top. And I can tell you, with one hundred percent honesty, that I haven't opened my legs to get where I'm at nor where I'm going."

He nearly covered his head at the verbal beating she was giving him. He hadn't meant the question like that and he certainly hadn't intended on insulting her in any way.

Things had been going so well, and then... *kaboom*...he had to make a misstep.

He should have just stayed quiet. Why hadn't he listened to himself?

"I'm sorry, Judge DeSalvo. I certainly didn't mean to question your..." He paused, unsure of exactly the words he should say: *reputation, womanhood, respect, honor, integrity?* None of them felt exactly right. But what had?

Ugh.

"You're fine." She didn't let him find the

word he had been looking for, but maybe that was for the best. He'd created a mess.

"No, really. I'm sorry." It was all he could think of to prove his sincerity. "The only reason I even approached that subject was out of necessity, not condescension. If there was any sort of romantic entanglement there, it means that there could also be some sort of third wheel complications that could happen."

"To be clear, you think that his wife would try to murder him and me?"

He pinched his lips together. Yes, that was exactly what it meant, but somehow it didn't seem like quite the right thing to say to her at the moment. Sometimes, when a person was at the bottom of a hole, it was best to stop digging.

"I'm just trying to narrow down the list of suspects. Who would want you dead, and why. That kind of thing." He had to question her thoroughly on this, but he'd wanted to wait until she was safe and somewhat recovered from the explosion.

She ran her hands over her face one more time, getting the last remnants of blood from her skin. There were tiny lines on her face, thin scratches like little hyphens.

He'd always prided himself on policing a world and helping it to run in an orderly fashion. He reduced violence and provided safety, so civilians and high-ranking officials could go about their business and function appropriately. And the woman beside him provided justice. Together, they made the world a place worth living.

What am I, Shakespeare now? he wondered. *What is she doing to me? I'm a door kicker, not a philosopher. I need to keep my head in the game.*

"I have never really had this kind of run-in before," she said, thankfully unaware of the weirdness that was happening in his mind. "I knew that I could run into this kind of problem eventually, but it's only been about a year since I have been on the bench. I thought I would be safe a little while longer."

"It is the moment you think you're safe, that you are at your most vulnerable. Your guard was down. I get it. I see it all the time. It's funny when guys have been in country for a long time. In the sandbox, they become desensitized and what would've freaked out a grunt becomes commonplace for them. I knew a guy who stood up in a bunker to take a picture for Instagram and got his head blown off. Complacency has always been humankind's worst enemy."

She nodded. "Working in the judicial system, I have to agree with you. Though I'm not sure if *complacency* is the right word. In my case, I think that narcissism is humankind's greatest enemy. People start to think that they can get away with anything if they are just smart enough."

He agreed with her there. The two parts often went hand in hand when it came to criminals. It was those who thought they were smarter than the rest of the world who grew bolder with time and lacked consequences for their terrible choices. Those choices grew darker, more nefarious, and they got what they wanted. Then they grew complacent and took things for granted. Sometimes they got caught, but not enough.

"Thinking about being complacent," he said, "you need to get rid of your cell phone. We can get you another one if you want, but for now you need to throw yours out on the interstate. Got it?"

Before he even finished speaking, the window was down and she was shoving the cell phone out.

"I wanted to do that with that stupid thing for years." She laughed, rolling up the window.

"I can only imagine."

"So where are you taking me? You had to have had some sort of plan for Judge Hanes in the event you guys had to bug out, right?" She paused. "Did I say that right, *bugging out*?"

"You can call it whatever you like, but in the end it all means getting the hell outta wherever you are. And no, I can't take you where I had planned on moving him to. Is there somewhere you think you would like to be taken? Somewhere you think it would be safe?"

She chewed her bottom lip, thinking. "There are always hotels?"

"Their databases are relatively easy to hack and if we use your credit card or my credit card, it would be pretty easy to track us down. We need something that won't leave a paper trail. How averse are you to spending a night out in the woods?"

She looked at him like he'd lost his mind. "You can't possibly think, for a single second, that I am camping." She motioned down to the clothes she was wearing. "This suit is a Dillard's finest—the best of the best in Montana. And if you think it is appropriate for sleeping outside, you are sorely mistaken. I'm more of a hotel girl. I need a hot shower and preferably a finger or two of vodka before I hit the sack."

Oh, I'd hit the sack with her, all right, he thought, then he realized what he had just let slip through the filter of his mind. *Shit. No. Job. Judge. Boundaries.*

His cheeks warmed. "You're right. No tents, no camping." No hitting of the sack…at least not together.

But if they couldn't go to a hotel and they couldn't camp, that left them with only a few options. They could go back to the STEALTH headquarters at the Widow Maker Ranch, but that would be the first place a hitman would look if they knew that Evan was involved.

"Up ahead, in just a few miles, is a little town," she said. "My pseudo-mom lives there and she would take us in. Her name is Judy."

"Would anyone think to look for you there?" he asked.

She shook her head. "Judy was my mother's best friend growing up, and when my mother died, she kind of filled her shoes. No one would know that but a select few. It is about the safest place I can think of."

"Tell me where to turn."

She nodded, and he could feel some of the tension slip away, momentarily. But as quickly as the pressure lifted, it was replaced with awkward silence.

But he could live in the silence.

Judge DeSalvo motioned at the next exit. "Turn here."

He followed her directions, but stayed quiet. She clasped her hands together tightly in her

lap; so tight that he could see that her finger-
nails were digging into the backs of her hands.
There were any number of things that could
have been bothering her, but he hated to assume or even talk about it. To talk about it and
give it air would only make them grow closer.
He couldn't want that.

"There is something about Judy," she said as
she moved her neck like she was trying to remove some kind of invisible noose. "She is a
worrier. If she hears about what has happened,
it will be a whole *thing*. I don't think it best that
we cause her any undue stress."

"So how do you want to handle showing up
at her door? Won't she ask questions? I don't
expect that you would normally just randomly
show up at her door on a weekday."

She nodded. "We talk once a week and I only
get to see her sporadically, when my schedule
allows. Which, as of late, has been very infre-
quently. In fact, I don't think I've come to see
her since I was elected. I've been horribly re-
miss in my duties as an honorary daughter."
There was the hint of guilt in her tone. "But
I'm hoping she won't ask too many questions
on how we found ourselves on her doorstep."

In theory, he could understand why she
would feel guilty, but since losing his own parents a few years ago he'd lost touch with what

exactly she had to be going through. The closest thing he had to even an adoptive parent
were his siblings. They had always gone out
of their way to make sure they worked as a
group, but the key word was *worked*. As members of the STEALTH team, they didn't mess
around with the touchy-feely things about family. Emotional wounds were left untouched so
they could knit naturally. None of them dared
to pick at the scabs.

"Anyway," Judge DeSalvo continued, "I
think it best if you just let me handle things
with her. Okay?"

"I didn't intend on anything else." He smiled.

She gave an appreciative nod. "Perfect."

"It may surprise you, but I'm pretty good
at just blending into the background." As he
spoke, he couldn't shut up the little voice in his
head that told him that the one place he wanted
to be was at the forefront of her life.

The little voice was an idiot.

Chapter Five

Judy was going to be beside herself with excitement. Or, at least she usually was when they got the opportunity to chat. Her second mom was always upbeat and full of life, fiery and wild in a way that made Natalie feel guilty for not having the same zest.

After her parents had died, some of what little zest she had been born with had slipped away. But even before, she had gone at life more linearly and methodically than the woman who had stepped in to raise her.

The last time she had seen Judy, she had flowers stuffed in her hair and an apron she had crocheted for collecting eggs from her bevy of chickens. And though she was in her late sixties, she was often mistaken for being at least two decades younger. If Natalie had to guess why, it was because of the unshaded light in her mother's eyes and the glorious smile that always rested on her lips.

It was strange, though, as Judy had lived a life full of tragedies. She had lost a daughter at birth and a son when he was thirteen in a boating accident, which had also taken her husband. Maybe it was tragedy that drew the two orphans together; their nearly perfect lives had been pulled out from under their feet.

Judy didn't focus on the past, though. She felt it, spoke about it and lived it, but she had moved forward with her life and it had grown no less dim. She was the most resilient and courageous woman that Natalie had ever known. If only she could be half as strong, she would be satisfied.

As Natalie pointed to the last house on the left, Evan pulled into the gravel driveway. The home was a simple, aged, single-story ranch house with three bedrooms and two bathrooms—one of which was still 1950s pink. It didn't seem to fit the bigger-than-life, grandiose Judy.

Natalie nibbled on her lip as she picked up her briefcase and he stopped the car. Walking around, he opened her door. "Ready for this?" Evan asked.

"As I will ever be," she said, suddenly nervous about what could come. She didn't want Judy to get upset. Sure, Judy could handle the news, but it would get blown completely out of proportion if she told her the truth. And she didn't want to lie, but white lies were made to keep people from getting hurt.

As she carried her briefcase up the askew concrete-slab sidewalk, she was brought back to the day she had first come to this house to live. Instead of a briefcase, she had been carrying her Winnie-the-Pooh suitcase, complete with a Piglet-shaped handle, though she had been sixteen.

Those had been some rough years, the time in life when a girl was expected to act like a woman but still had the mind of a girl. But she had grown up fast. She had only gone on one date by the time she was a senior in high school. And yet, even without the complication of first love and first heartbreak, there were many growing pains that had come in the years she had lived in this little house.

How had she found herself feeling just as scared and lost as she had when she was sixteen and walking up this walkway with Piglet in hand? The only thing that had changed was the kind of bag she carried and the start of crow's feet at the corners of her eyes.

The front door opened and Judy flung herself in her direction before Natalie's foot had even hit the bottom step. "Natty! You didn't tell me you were coming! What are you doing here?" she squealed with delight as she threw her arms around Natalie's neck.

Natalie laughed into her mother's gray hair. No flowers today. But she did have a large red-tailed hawk feather poking out of her braid in the back. Knowing her, it was probably a feather she had found somewhere in the woods on her daily hike. Judy had always found beauty in nature and celebrated the littlest things.

And then there was Natalie, not even calling her before showing up on her doorstep. She was a terrible daughter. Here was the woman who had practically raised her after some of the hardest years of her life, a woman who could be satisfied with the littlest signs of appreciation and love, and she had brought her nothing.

"Hi, Mom, sorry. I should have called."

Judy gave her a kiss on the cheek and backed up, holding her by the shoulders and inspecting her. "You haven't been eating enough, and you look like you've been through the wringer. What happened?"

Natalie shot Evan a look before answering. "Nothing. Just took a tumble. I'm fine."

"Come in. I just made fresh fry bread. You and your friend here can pour some cinnamon and sugar on it and fatten yourselves up." She turned around and motioned them inside.

It shouldn't have surprised Natalie that Judy

hadn't even batted an eyelash about her feeble explanation of her injuries or her bringing a stranger to her house—and not just any stranger, but an incredibly good-looking one. She had called him "her friend," which meant she must have assumed there was some kind of relationship between them, and in doing so she was clearly assuming that Natalie could bat in the same league that this man played in. She did not.

Evan opened the door and waited for them to enter. He gave her a confused look, like he wondered if it was just normal that a stranger would walk right into their house without so much as a simple introduction. *Oh, Judy.*

As Natalie walked by him, she made sure to take a quick glance at his ass. It was just as tight and muscular as the rest of him, and it solidly cinched the fact that he was too much of a man for her. If she had to bet on it, not that she was a betting woman, she would have put money on the probability that he dated model types. The last kind of woman he would be after would be one who was most comfortable in a beautiful black muumuu robe. The collar was nice, though. Maybe he had a collar fetish.

She chuckled at the thought as she stepped around him and went inside.

Though she couldn't turn around without

being conspicuous, she was sure that she could feel his gaze trailing down her backside. She smiled at the thought. Maybe it was just wishful thinking.

She sucked in a breath, trying to collect herself.

If merely the disparity in looks wasn't a problem, there was also the fact that they lived and operated in entirely different worlds. He was the kind of man who came so close to breaking the law that he put cracks in it, while she was the one who was forced to come behind people like him and patch up the holes and repair the damage.

Yes, if they were friends at the end of this it would be a miracle. Actually, if he came out of this without her putting him in jail for breaking laws, she would be impressed. He had already skirted around procedures by sneaking her out of a crime scene before she could give a statement to law enforcement, something she needed to rectify.

She grumbled slightly as she thought about all the work she would have to do when she went back to Missoula. Things were going to be a mess, but at least she wouldn't have to worry about any trials for the rest of the week.

"Why the face?" Judy asked, looking at her as they made their way into the kitchen.

She forced a smile, even though she knew her second mom would see right through it. "Nothing. I was just thinking."

"Well, at some point I hope you do enough thinking to tell me how you got so beat-up looking. Must have been some fall you took." She gave Natalie a once-over. "I don't know how you do what you do, lady. So exhausting. And oh, the things you must see every day—I can't even imagine," she said, pulling a plate of fresh fry bread out of the oven and setting it on the island with a shaker of sugar and cinnamon. "I hope your friend here knows what a catch he has gotten in you. You are quite the woman."

Natalie could feel the fire rise in her cheeks. Judy may not have been her mother by blood, but she didn't miss a beat in acting like she was—especially when it came to embarrassing her.

"Did you know that Natty graduated first in her class and was valedictorian in her high school? She is a smart cookie."

"Yes, ma'am," Evan said, finally piping up. "I didn't know she was valedictorian, but knew from the first moment I saw her that she was an incredible woman. I feel lucky to have her even grace me with her presence."

What in the hell was he playing at?

"Mom, Evan is—"

Judy waved her to a stop. "Shush now, Evan and I are discussing you. Just listen in and take the compliments."

She clenched her teeth, the muscles in her jaw protruding. Her mom knew exactly how much she hated being the center of attention, especially when accolades were being awarded. She would much rather have been getting yelled at by a defendant and telling them to stand down—at least there she could be in control.

"I hope your intentions are pure with our girl here," Judy continued.

Natalie sent Evan a look that said "get us out of here" in a thousand languages. Yet, he pitched his head back with a laugh. "I can tell you, ma'am, I'll be nothing if not a gentleman when it comes to your daughter."

Judy took him by the arm and led him to the plate. She nearly fed him herself after she fussed about a piece of bread and held it to him. He seemed to be soaking it all in with a level of aplomb that even Queen Elizabeth would have been proud of.

Judy whispered something to Evan she couldn't quite hear, but it made her even more uncomfortable. Knowing her, it could have been a threat against his life if he hurt her, or a promise of cookies and cakes if he was a good boy. Though Natalie was fine with her mother saying either, she wished she could at least hear so she could talk about it with Evan later and make sure he understood that whatever Judy said, it was coming from a place of love.

There was a reason Natalie had never brought a man here before. Not even when she had been dating had she wanted to bring them within a hundred yards of this house. Her mom was a wonderful woman, but she could get attached quickly. Attachment would lead to entanglements and when the relationship ended, which they always did, it would be even harder to disengage if Judy harbored feelings, as well.

Natalie glanced down at her watch. It was about an hour back to the city; if they left now, she could be back to her own bed at her regular time—death threats be damned.

"You know, Natty, looking at your watch when we have guests is rude."

And there she was, put right back into her sixteen-year-old shoes, being chastised by her favorite larger-than-life woman.

"Sorry, I was just—"

Again, she was waved off. "I know, I know." Judy sighed. "I will put together the back bedroom for you two. I assume you will be sleeping in the same room?"

Holy crap, way to cut right to the quick of things.

"Judy, Mom—"

"Ms. Judy," Evan jumped in, "for the respect of your house, if it is at all possible, I think it best if we slept in separate rooms. We wouldn't want any of your friends to think you were anything but a moral, upstanding woman."

Judy laughed, hard. "Oh my goodness. We don't live in Victorian times. And I couldn't give two figs about what any old biddies have to say. If they have a problem with how I live my life, they can take it up with me. Or not. My response will be the same."

He glanced over at her and Natalie shrugged. There were some things and some fights that Judy was never going to let others win, and she had a feeling that this was one of those spars.

"You go and grab your bags and I'll pull everything together." In true Judy fashion, she left them in a flurry of feathers and spice.

It was quiet for the first time since they had stepped on the property. The only sounds were of Judy talking to herself as she made her way down the hallway and to the linen closet.

Natalie let out a long exhale. "I should have warned you. She is a bit of a hurricane in person, but I swear she leaves things better than she found them."

"Then I would hardly call that a hurricane."

"Fire, then?"

He tilted his head back and forth like he was letting the idea roll around in his mind, and the effect was even more endearing than she could have imagined. "I'll allow it. And I can see her ripping through any forest and leaving only ashes and wildflowers behind her."

Natalie laughed. "I'm sorry that she seems to think we're dating. I'll make sure to set things straight with her. And I will get us separate bedrooms."

Just the thought of having to sleep next to this handsome, charming man made her no-no places clench. She had incredible restraint when it came to men and to falling to the needs of her body, but she wasn't sure that she would be as strong if she could hear his breath in the still of the night. And if he touched her, game over.

Yes, they definitely needed separate bedrooms. Better yet, they could go back to the city. Yes, the city.

"Ms. Judy seems to be soaking it all up. I think she likes the idea of us being together."

And I don't mind it, either. Her mind raced, but she checked it. *Don't be an idiot, woman. Slow your roll.*

"That doesn't mean we should allow her to keep assuming, incorrectly, that we are something we are not."

"But what does it hurt? In fact, it's a lot easier letting her believe you brought me here to meet her than telling her we had to run here after someone tried to murder you."

She paused. "You have a point."

But there had to be some kind of happy medium that didn't involve any kind of interrogations about relationships or loss of life. In truth, she didn't know which was worse when it came to having a conversation with her mom.

"If it makes you feel better, I will sleep on the floor and you can have the bed."

"Are you sure we shouldn't head back to Missoula?" she asked, biting the inside of her cheek as she envisioned him shirtless on the floor beside her. "Besides, we didn't even bring bags. You don't think my mom will notice?"

He looked at her and sent her a sexy half grin. "You forget—I'm damn near a Boy Scout den leader here. I'm always prepared. I got my go-bag in the truck." He went to retrieve it.

She found herself standing alone in the kitchen, staring down at the plate of warm carbs, as everyone around her was going out of their way to make sure she was comfortable and taken care of. Lucky; she was incredibly lucky.

But how had her life gone from sitting on the bench and making life and death decisions for others to standing in her mom's kitchen and making life and death decisions for herself?

She stuffed a piece of bread into her mouth, closing her eyes as the sugar melted on her tongue. What was the world trying to tell her in forcing her to do this, to be here?

Maybe it was a little too ethereal, and she should have been focusing on the danger that she faced, but what if the world or the fates had a plan for her? She didn't believe in coincidence. Everything a person did in their lives, every decision they made, led them to a place they were meant to be. But what had led her here?

Slipping on a coat Judy had hanging on a peg, she walked through the kitchen and stepped out the back door. The sun was starting to set and she sat down on the fence-rail swing in the center of the yard. She rocked as she ate the last of her bread and stared at the pinks and oranges glowing on the mountaintops that were covered with snow.

It felt wrong to relax, to be enjoying the beauty of nature and life when the world was threatening to burn down around her, but at the same time it felt right to just take time and breathe it all in. Maybe that was the purpose of this, to focus on living the moments that were granted to her—who knew how many she would have left? The thought made her heart lurch. What would it mean to be taken from this earth? And why? What reason would someone have to hate her enough to want to snuff out her life?

Every day she had to face herself in the mirror and answer for the choices and decisions she made when it came to people's lives. She always tried to do the right thing, to follow the laws, directives and choices that others before her had made. Life was built of injustices— most couldn't be made right. The vast majority of the tragedies in this life didn't happen due to random acts of nature, but choices. It could be as simple as making the decision to get in a car or to say yes when a person should say no. It was these simple moments that ruined lives and wrought injustice and mayhem.

It was the sands of mistakes that built up to create the speed bumps in life.

She sighed, soaking in the sunset as it billowed from yellows and pinks to purples and grays. Soon, the stars would come. Turning to her right, she could see Polaris shining in the distance. It was always there to guide her, no matter what was happening in her life. This wasn't a mistake. She was here for a reason.

She had once read a line in Philipp Meyer's *The Son*, which went something like: "May the stars shine so bright it is impossible to sleep." Tonight she felt those words' pull. The stars were bright.

It was odd how dancing the line between life and death could make a person feel more alive. There must have been something wrong with her that she found a modicum of joy and beauty in this moment.

There was the screech of the screen door as it opened and closed, but she didn't turn around. Whomever wanted her dead wouldn't find her here; only those who wished her alive.

Evan sat down next to her, touching her as they rocked in silence. He handed her a drink, and she took a sip. Iced tea. Her first of the year. Just another symbolic change in her life. Winter was heavy, but spring was taking root. Until now she had been in the winter of her life—living only to survive, but brought to a point today when survival was literal instead of just figurative. Was this her moment to spring? To revel in the stars and grow?

She had forgotten how beautiful life could be.

She couldn't recall the last time she had taken time to sit and watch the sunset turn into the stars.

Evan put his arm behind her on the bench.

"Are you doing okay? I know something like this can take a toll on a person."

She nodded, careful to keep from touching him, as if it would bring them too close too fast; or maybe his touch would bring back the reality of her life and break the spell the natural world had placed upon her.

"Judy caught me inside. She said she was heading to bed, but she would see us in the morning." He smiled, his teeth sparkling in the thin light.

"What?" She had never known her mother to be an early-to-bed kind of woman.

"Yep," he said with a chuckle. "And she also said that she would make sure to have plenty of protein to 'rejuvenate' us in the morning."

"Oh. My. God. She didn't." Natalie nearly splashed her tea on her shirt as she moved to cover her face in embarrassment.

"Oh, she did." He laughed loud and long. "Your mom is freaking awesome."

There were any number of words she could think of to describe Judy right now—obtrusive, meddlesome—but the last that came to mind was *awesome*.

"I'm glad you brought us here. If anything it is making me laugh. Right now I appreciate a little lightheartedness. It's not something you often find hours after a murder attempt." His hand moved down and his fingers trailed on the top of her shoulder.

His gentle touch moved in time with the swing and as it did, it was like he was thrumming the strings of her soul.

"You know," he continued, "I am here if you need to talk about what happened back there. I know how hard it can be and all the things that can go through a person's mind when something like that happens."

She glanced over at him, staring at his green eyes. They were picking up the gray of the sky, making him look stormy.

"I appreciate your concern, but I really am doing okay. More than anything, I am just at a loss. I can't think of a concrete reason anyone would want me dead."

He thrummed harder. "Are you sure?"

She nodded, but all she was really thinking about was his fingers on her. "Wait… Do you have your phone?" she asked, holding out her hand, expectantly.

He scowled, the look making it clear that he wasn't the kind of person who would just willingly hand over his private information. And yet, he reached into his back pocket and pulled it out. He didn't hand it over. "What are you thinking?"

She wanted to just show him, but she honored his privacy and dropped her hand. There wasn't a chance in hell she would have handed her phone over to a stranger without any sort of context, either. "Pull up Instagram and type in the judge's son's name."

"Why do you want to look him up?" Evan asked.

She shrugged. "It seems like the most obvious place to start looking. I know he and his son are close, but Sven has a history. And, if nothing else, at least we can cross him off our list." And she could think about something besides the way Evan's touch felt, even through her coat.

He moved closer and started clicking on the phone with the hand that was wrapped around her shoulders, and the action drew her closer into him. So close, in fact, that she could smell the cinnamon on his breath and the smoky residue of the car bomb on his skin. It was a strange combination, the spice and the danger, but it was an oddly heady mix. She closed her eyes as he clicked and she drew in a long breath of him.

The timing of this crush couldn't have been more off. She yearned to dance with this Devil, and yet a different manner of hell was threatening her world.

He typed in *Sven Hanes Missoula*.

"There," she said, pointing at his profile.

Evan opened it up; thankfully, it wasn't set on private. The last picture that Sven had posted was tagged at a restaurant in Kennewick, Washington. It was a simple photo, nothing more than a long-necked beer and a burger, but it put him hours from the crime scene when the attack had happened.

But just because a person tagged themselves at a place, didn't mean they were actually there. For all she knew, he could have been standing behind them now. Social media wasn't known for its accurate representations of real life.

Sven could very well have posted something tagged in another state, just to throw anyone who thought he was behind the attacks off his scent.

"Hmm," she said, pinching her lips together.

"Have you had any cases that were out of the ordinary lately? Something that involved both you and Judge Hanes? We're going to have to go over this, but I wanted you to have some space first."

"Our caseloads don't usually overlap. He has his dockets and I have mine." She mulled over his question for a long moment. "But…on occasion we have lawyers and their clients who are all about playing games, and some who think one judge would be better suited for hearing their case than another. In fact, that happens quite a bit in complicated cases."

"Has it happened in the last few weeks?"

She nodded. "A few of those filings have floated over my desk, but I can think of one that surprised me… I don't have the details, but it was an odd case. It was marked assault libel and slander—not abnormal, except it was between two women. I thought I would be sitting on the bench. Any sort of cases involving women's rights are normally run by me. The local attorneys know that I am more of an advocate. However, this one they moved to Hanes."

"Did he hear the case, or did it end up being settled?"

"Strangely enough, he did—two days before the attacks."

His eyebrows rose. "What happened?"

"Like I said, I don't know the particulars, but I know Judge Hanes had a hard time with that ruling—he drank nearly a half bottle of scotch with me that evening. He mentioned that the defendant had to be taken away by the bailiff after finding herself in contempt of court. Apparently, she thought it was okay to try and climb up over the bench and attempt to punch Hanes." She let out a half chuckle. "At the time, we both shrugged it off. Most people don't come at the judge—they will yell at us, call us every name under the sun, but there is generally some sort of internal stop point before people try to physically assault us in the middle of the courtroom."

"I think you may well be on to something with this defendant—we need to look into her. You said she was found in contempt of court. Was she out of jail today?"

"She just had to pay a fine and she was released." Natalie shifted slightly and Evan sat back, releasing her from his hold. The cool night air swirled in and pulled the warmth away from where he had been touching her.

"Do you know anything about the case? Maybe the woman's name?"

"The case was Sanders vs. Rencher. When Hanes and I chatted afterward, he said it had to do with a custody agreement that had gone wrong. The two women had been married, but are getting divorced. They had shared custody of a child, but something happened and somehow the two women ended up in a fight. Sanders ended up threatening to kill the other, and it is my understanding that she nearly finished the job."

"Well, at least it wasn't a murder case."

"If the police hadn't interceded at the right time, I think it would have been." She understood rage, but had never understood how another person could murder someone they had once loved. "Regardless, if we are going down the list of who would be capable of taking us out, she would be one of the most recent suspects. There is nothing more dangerous than a pissed off mother."

Chapter Six

His boss, Zoey Martin, was not pleased when he called. He wasn't surprised. Zoey wasn't known for her softness, even after she'd gotten pregnant. If anything, she'd grown more cantankerous over the past few months. Even though she had grumbled and cussed when he had let her know all that had transpired, she had eventually validated his actions and agreed to send someone in to stand by Judge Hanes's hospital room and ensure his safety as well as try to get more info when he was responsive.

By the end of the conversation, she had even commended him for his quick action in treating the judge. Her praise was as rare as her smile, so he graciously accepted what she chose to give.

She'd also sent him all the records she could find on the case Natalie had mentioned as well as everything she could locate about both judges—including links to all their rulings—

and even Hanes's marriage license. He chuckled as he thought about how little use he would see coming from that particular piece of paper. In his life, the ink used to print the document had been worth more than what it stood for.

He wasn't sure he would ever really like to get married again. Screw that. Love had only ever led to heartache and resentment. He preferred sitting in a Humvee in the middle of a war zone and taking rounds than having to navigate the minefield that was a relationship.

No doubt this Sanders woman likely had felt the same way. According to the court records, she and her wife had been in a tempestuous relationship with verbal and physical disagreements so bad that the police had been called out several times. Once, her partner had been slapped with an assault charge after Rencher had gone after Sanders with a knife. According to the police report of that incident, Rencher had said the incident with the knife had resulted from self-defense.

Sanders had brought the assault up in Hanes's courtroom, but in the end, Hanes had ruled against Sanders. That was odd. His ruling didn't make sense. Sanders was clearly the victim. And according to the documents in his hands, she should have won her case against Rencher for assault. Was there something here that he wasn't seeing? He had all of the records and the court reporter's full file, and no matter how many times he read through it, he couldn't understand Hanes's ruling.

He shook his head.

As he read deeper and deeper into the case, he wondered what Natalie would have made of it.

He glanced over at her as she slept peacefully in the bed. She wore pajamas she'd found in a dresser in the room. She'd been delighted to see there were things she could wear today. She must not have changed much since she'd lived here.

They'd talked briefly about her cases, and he planned on asking her more about other rulings, jogging her memory with the links Zoey had sent. Somewhere in her past was someone who'd been angry enough to lash out at her and Judge Hanes.

He had been more than happy to take the floor and keep the peace between the two women of the house. It made him laugh every time he thought about Natalie's matron. Judy was a hoot. Though he could tell that she embarrassed the hell out of Natalie.

That made him miss his own mom. She had died several years ago in a car accident, along with his father. He had never really gotten over their loss. There were so many things that they would never get to be a part of, so many things they wouldn't be able to enjoy—if only his mom could be teasing him the same way Judy teased them.

Judy would have made a great mother-in-law. Not that he was ever going to get back into a relationship.

He was tough, incredibly so, but when it came to being with a woman, he was too tenderhearted. Whenever he had fallen in love in the past it was like he had always chosen the one being who he knew he shouldn't have. His ex-wife had been completely different from Natalie. Maybe as strong but that was where the similarities ended. His ex had told him that all she ever really wanted was to be alone; he had run up against it and fought to earn a place in her life. For a while, it had worked.

They had loved each other. Or he had assumed they had loved one another, and then she didn't want him anymore.

He couldn't begrudge her for putting herself first, for fighting to be at peace with herself, but he couldn't stop himself from being hurt. He had offered her a part of himself, which he rarely gave to anyone, and it hadn't been enough.

She wasn't the one for him; logically, he realized that. But when the heart said something was right and the mind said "you're being stupid," it was crazy how often the heart won. From here on out, he was listening to his brain. It knew better, and perhaps it could save him from himself—if he was lucky and if he actually listened.

Then again, he had never been known for his emotional intelligence. Far from it.

Natalie sighed in her sleep and his heart flipped in his chest, like her subtle little noise had somehow jump-started the poor, wretched beast.

Down, boy.

This fight with the mind wasn't going to be as easy as he'd hoped. And really, how was this time with Natalie any different than before? Here he was, forced to be close to a woman he was protecting, a woman who was entirely off-limits. All he had to do was keep his distance.

It will get easier as soon as I'm out of this house.

Yep, that was it. It was just that they were too close. He leaned up against the bed, turning his back to her so he wouldn't be tempted to look up at the beautiful woman once again.

Maybe it was just harder than normal because they were pretending to be in a relationship that they couldn't really be in. In the past, when he'd been forced to go undercover, he'd adopted mannerisms and qualities of the characters he was playing, going so deep that he became them. Maybe that was exactly what was happening here. He was loving her because he was pretending to love her. Nothing more.

Yep, that had to be it.

Finally, a bit of relief drifted through him. If nothing else, he had a reason and an answer for the confusing feelings that were working through him.

Maybe he needed to take a page from his ex's playbook and just be alone.

He nodded to himself and as he did, Natalie's fingers touched him. He glanced back at her sleeping face. As he moved, she reached into his hair, stroking his head. She sighed as she ran her fingers through his locks. He moved into her touch like a soft, well-broken horse. Even if she was only pretending to be asleep, his longing to be touched like that outweighed the need to protect his heart and pull away.

When he woke up the next morning, his phone was on the floor next to his head, and at some point someone must have covered him with a pink rose-covered blanket. Though he was getting older with each passing day, when he sat up his body didn't hurt too badly even though he had been smooshed into the carpet fibers all night long. He rolled onto his back. Natalie's hand was hanging limply over the bed above him. Her nails were long and perfectly manicured. Did she pay to get them done, or did she sit at home once a week and do them herself?

He looked at his own nails. They were worn short and there was dirt and what he betted was spent gunpowder under their edges. The base of his thumb had a nice callus from his days spent on the gun range.

There were no calluses on her hands. No dirt. No blisters from manual labor or backbreaking tasks. Her tasks only broke the soul.

He definitely didn't envy her work. But then, she probably would say the same thing about his.

They were never to be. They were too different.

He scratched at his nose, pulling off a piece of fuzz that had stuck to his face in the night.

There was a knock on the door. "Wake up, kids. Breakfast is ready," Judy said, calling in.

Natalie's hand disappeared. "All right. We will be out in a minute," she said, sounding sleepy.

Damn, only this woman could make mornings sexy. His body had its own mind and as he thought of her and of waking up alongside her, it rose to greet the day.

Or maybe he had just been lonely too long. Or maybe it was just morning. *Get it together, dumbass*.

He moved to his feet, careful to keep his back turned to her. The last thing he needed to have was for her to see where his mind was and for him to see her tussled hair and makeup-less face. She was probably even more beautiful in her natural state. Women never believed that, but he loved it when a woman was comfortable enough to show her true self to him.

And yet, she was probably sitting there all worried about what she looked like and feeling insecure. They had been pushed into this; there was nothing about it that had come naturally—except the pull he felt to be closer to her.

"You can turn around. I'm not naked," she said, half laughing.

He wasn't sure exactly what to say, so he went with the first thing that came to mind. "Sorry, your morning breath… Damn, woman, let me get you a toothbrush."

She punched him squarely in the right butt cheek, not hard enough to hurt but just enough to get his attention.

"Hey, now," he said, turning around. "Most women have to pay to touch that."

She laughed. "What are you, a stripper or something?"

"I swear I'm only putting myself through college," he teased, doing a little dance move that made it look like he was twirling a feather boa. He hummed a bawdy song as he tapped his foot.

She laughed, the sound bouncing off the walls. Her joy tore at his resolve, clawing its way through his self-built barricades.

She moved to the edge of the bed and sat up, her legs on each side of his. "Oh, yeah," she said, laughing as she pretended to flip money at him. "I'll make it rain."

He put his hands behind his head and did a hip shake in front of her.

"Oh la la," she said, but somehow as she put her hands up, he moved into her and her hand grazed against his morning's gift. "Oh. Hey. Um. I'm. Yeah…" Her cheeks turned crimson.

He stumbled on his feet as he fell backward, slamming against the wall behind him. "Crap," he said, trying to right himself and gain control over what his body had gotten him into. "I'm sorry. It's my fault. I didn't mean to—"

They both sat there staring at one another for a long moment. She couldn't have been as embarrassed as he was, and yet, from the color of her face, he was sure that she was.

"I...you..." she started, but stopped.

There was no getting out of this uncomfortable moment; it was best to just acknowledge it. "Yeah, now you are really going to have to lay down some money. That is like VIP room treatment right there." He laughed in an attempt to cover his unease. "Here, let's get you dressed. I need coffee before you use me for my body again."

Her eyes widened in surprise and she opened her mouth. He didn't know why he did it—maybe it was the laughter on her lips or the joy he felt when he looked into her eyes, but he leaned in and kissed her. She didn't move away, as he expected. Maybe she was just as surprised as he was; this wasn't something he had meant to do. It wasn't something he had even thought about doing, at least not in any real way, and yet, here he was...her tongue glazing over his bottom lip.

She ran her hands over his ass, pulling him into her. She ran her hands up his back, her action forceful, and he felt himself submitting to her will. It felt backward, like he should have been the one to take charge and lead the advance, but at the same time he liked this relinquishing of power. There was something so immeasurably sexy about a woman who took what she wanted and had the confidence to make her wishes known.

She leaned back, not breaking their kiss as she pulled him down on top of her in the bed.

He moved against her, her body answering in kind. His lips trailed down her neck and he unbuttoned her pajama top, revealing her naked breasts. Cupping them, he stared. Her nipples were the color of toffee and, as he popped one in his mouth, they tasted just as sweet. He licked at the nub then rubbed it over his lips like he was marking it as his, yes…forever his.

She arched her back and as she did, her nipple grazed the stubble around his lips and she gasped. He ran his hand down her body, feeling the subtle curves of her stomach and the crests of her hip. Searching for her warmth, the heat drew him in until his fingers found what he yearned to find. He would taste that next.

Rubbing against her, his mouth found her nipple again and he sucked until her breath caught in her throat and he could feel the heat grow under his fingertips. Her wetness soaked through the thin cotton of her pajamas. He lowered his touch, dipping into her, and she lifted her hips to meet him. Trailing his kisses down her stomach, he found her navel. Stopping for a moment, he ran his finger around the indentation.

He'd never thought of a navel as sexy before, but there was no place on her body he didn't want to see and make his. His heart beat for her, and if she let him, it would beat for her forever.

"You're right," she said, touching his hands. "We should stop."

Holy shit, that had been the furthest thing from his mind. How had she gotten there? All he wanted to do was pull every piece of clothing from her body and make love to her until there was nothing left of him to give.

"Uh," he said, trying to compose himself.

She moved and he rolled off her. It physically pained him to move from between her legs. It was like he had finally found a place that he wanted to call home and it was being ripped from his grasp.

"I…"

"I know," she said, stealing his words. "Judy is holding breakfast for us. And I agree that this isn't a great idea—for a variety of reasons."

Damn. She wasn't wrong, but that didn't make his need for her dissipate.

What hadn't he done right that she wanted to pull away from his touch? Hell, that she *could* pull away from his touch? Should he have moved his fingers faster? Should he never have stopped to look at her? Should he have devoured her before she had a moment to collect herself?

He leaned back, adjusting himself. Nope. He respected her boundaries. Hell, maybe he needed to put his up with steel and stone.

Standing up, he moved away from her and smoothed his hair. He ran his hand over his normally well-groomed beard, like it was the reason she had pushed him away. Maybe he needed to shave it off. He nearly shook his head at the thought; he wasn't giving up his beard. He couldn't make her want him, but he could stop himself from giving up his facial security blanket.

Before he got any more stupid ideas, he walked to the door. "I'll meet you down there. Coffee? Cream and sugar?"

"Yes, please. Just black."

Yep, she was far stronger than he was, though he would never dare to admit that aloud to her. They had to have an equal position of respect if they were ever going to try these kinds of shenanigans again. Maybe that was why she had stopped the advance; maybe she had realized she was about nine miles outside his league. He wouldn't blame her if she had figured that one out, but until he was sure that she had, he had to try and keep himself in the game.

He made his way down the hall, giving himself a moment to let things settle before he saw Judy. He didn't need her noticing anything that would make her suspicions about their relationship, burgeoning or otherwise, rise to the surface.

As he approached the kitchen, he was met with the scents of hot coffee, pancakes and bacon.

How had Natalie ever wanted to leave this heaven?

If this was what he had every day, he would just curl up on the couch and never leave.

Okay, maybe that was a little extreme. He did love his job. There was little better than taking out a threat who put those whom he loved and cared about—or was paid to care about—in danger. He was the world's checks and balances in human form, and with that came an incredible sense of identity and self.

"Good morning, ma'am," he said, making his way around the corner and into the main room.

Judy was humming away as she did something in the sink and she turned at the sound of his voice. "Good morning. I bet you are hungry. Are you a bacon or sausage guy? What's your favorite?"

"My favorite is anything you are about to feed me. Seriously, I'm not picky. Just grateful."

Judy beamed. "Smart man."

"I wouldn't go so far as to say that, but I would say hungry," he said with a mischievous grin.

She dried her hands and came over and gave him a quick peck on the cheek. The simple action caught him off guard; there was something so European and old-worldly about it that it made him like this wonderful woman even more.

"Before my daughter gets down here, I want you to know something about her."

He wanted to know everything, but he was surprised that she would want to help him. Not sure exactly what to say, he nodded.

She looked up at him, studying his eyes for a long moment before giving him a little nod. "I can tell you guys are new to each other. But there is something you need to know about her, if you want to keep her…" Judy looked over her shoulder as if she was checking to make sure that Natalie hadn't somehow snuck up from behind. "Natalie has been through some hard times. Incredibly hard. But her spirit gets her through. She is like wildfire… You either run with her or you will be consumed."

He didn't doubt that for a second.

"I think you need to know, we aren't—"

"Dating? Oh, I know. I could tell," Judy said with a wicked smile. "But that doesn't mean that there isn't something between you two. I can feel it. And I know you can feel it. It is my job, as a parent figure, to make sure that my daughter gets the best things in life." She grabbed the bacon plate and slid it toward him on the counter. "Now, you just eat up. Let me worry about the rest."

He took a piece of bacon and stuffed it into his mouth. No matter what he said or thought, he could see that he would be quickly outvoted by the spark plug of a woman. From what he could tell, the warning she had given him about Natalie could have easily been applied to herself—maybe Natalie had become like the woman who'd raised her.

Whatever had caused it, he was honored to be even a minimal part of their experiences in life.

That was all he had ever really wanted to be, decor in other people's lives. Most people wouldn't understand this desire, the want to never hold a key role. It was easier to be in on the sidelines, acting as the guard. It was so much easier than actually being forced to feel. To feel made a person real, exposed, raw. It was crazy that Natalie made him want to step into a real role again. Maybe it was just the pull of her lips that had drawn him to her. Maybe it had just been too long since he had been that close to a woman. But as quickly as that thought came to his mind, he brushed it away. She wasn't just any woman. She was something truly special—she was smart, strong and level-headed. She was everything he had ever wanted.

He couldn't put his finger on exactly what it was that made him want to be raw and exposed when it came to her. Until he could figure out what drew him in, he needed to stay emotionally away—or at least at arm's length. He wouldn't leave her alone in her moment of need, not when he had the ability to be exactly what she needed to stay safe.

Natalie walked into the kitchen, pulling a white sweater over her head and then patting down her hair, making sure every piece was solidly in place in her ponytail. As she strode over to the plate of bacon he was taken aback—how had he gotten so lucky to have tasted her and felt her warmth on his fingers? He couldn't help but feel like the luckiest, albeit most confused, man in the world.

She smothered her pancakes in so much warm maple syrup that he considered telling her to just grab a bowl of syrup and crumble some pancake on top, but then he followed her lead.

Judy walked to the refrigerator and took out

a can of whipped cream and handed it to her, like this breakfast was some sort of routine the two ladies had been choreographing for years. It was their dance, elegant and smooth, just like the women it belonged to.

She reminded him of a swan. When they fell in love, they did a beautiful dance of head bobs and spins. Suddenly, he wanted to take her in his arms and sweep her around the kitchen, dancing with her in a way that only they could. And yet, such a motion seemed out of place and gauche in their graceful world.

He would always be the door kicker in this world of ballerinas.

Judy was conspicuously quiet as they all sat around and ate; in fact, they barely said a word until each had drunk a full cup of coffee.

Maybe that, too, was part of their routine.

If it was, he loved them both more for it.

Finally, Natalie pushed her plate away and spoke up. "I don't know about you, Evan, but I need to get back to the city. Would you mind running me home so I can pick up a few things? Then we can come back here, if that's okay with you?" She looked at Judy.

The older woman sent him a look, but he didn't know exactly what to make of the question in her eyes.

"I would rather we stay here. I mean, what do

you really need that we can't find at a store?"
He tried to send Natalie a look that said there
was no freaking way that this would be a good
idea—the last thing they should do is stick her
head out of the safety of their temporary den.,

He still needed to go through the list of past
cases with her more thoroughly, especially the
one that had landed in Hanes's courtroom.

She didn't look at him.

Did this sudden need to run away from this
place have something to do with what had happened between them in her bedroom?

Damn it, he had been so stupid. What had he
been thinking in going in for that kiss? Right,
he hadn't been.

This was exactly the kind of nonsense that
happened when a person went along with the
needs of their body over the requirements of
their lives. He had obligations, to his team, to
his family and to her. He had compromised
his objectives by acting as foolishly as he had.

Maybe if they went back to the city, he could
call in one of his teammates and they could
take over this security detail…for no money,
and out of the goodness of their hearts. After
all, it was Hanes who'd originally brought him
in, and they were protecting the judge in his
hospital room.

He gritted his teeth. Zoey had been behind

his helping her; hopefully she could convince someone else from his team to help. A.J. had always been the philanthropist. He would probably step up if he was called.

He should have known that Natalie wasn't emotionally available, and maybe he wasn't, either.

Yeah, that was it. Emotionally unavailable. Wall up. Dick off. Life back to normal. He set his jaw.

"You guys are welcome to come and go as you please," Judy said, sending them each a smile, but her eyes lingered on Natalie. "I think you should stay here as long as your work allows, Natty. I think you need a bit of a break. You are looking a little overwhelmed this morning, even if you did clean up all those scratches I saw yesterday."

Natalie huffed into her coffee cup as she moved to take a sip. "It was a long night."

Judy laughed, making a blush rise in his cheeks he wished he could control. And yet, just like these two women, his body's response seemed to have a mind of its own. Damn if he didn't love them for it, but hate himself for it at the same time.

"Yeah, maybe it's best if we head back." He could sit here and argue why they shouldn't leave all morning, but the woman of fire was always going to get her way. It was better to have a plan in place for what she needed instead of trying to impose his will. Even if he was the type, it wouldn't have worked.

He downed his coffee and put the empty cup in the sink. "Thank you for having us, ma'am. I hope to see you again." He gave Judy a wink and she answered with a sad, reconciled smile. "Natalie, I will meet you outside."

It felt like he was running away, but he couldn't handle all the feelings that were whirling around in the kitchen. A moment later he grabbed his wallet and the truck keys from beside the bed, made a quick trip to the bathroom, and by the time he was walking outside he noted Natalie was already there, briefcase in hand.

Apparently, she was in a bigger rush to get out of here than he was.

Judy was nowhere to be seen.

He had no idea what to say, or how he should approach the judge. All he wanted to do was to apologize and tell her that lust had clouded his judgment and the pheromones had reared their ugly heads, but would be kept under better control.

"You and Judy make quite the pair," he said, making his way out toward her.

Yes, innocuous…it was his only play.

She looked at him and frowned. Had she expected him to just come out and talk about what had transpired between them, or had she been preparing for him to argue the point that they should have stayed at the little farm?

He went into instinct mode, viewing the area around his truck. His scan started at twenty feet out, then ten, and finally five. It was something he always did anytime he got in or out of a vehicle. It was an old habit he had picked up over the pond. Nothing appeared amiss at twenty feet or ten, but when he glanced at the ground near the driver's-side door, the dirt had been scuffed.

It could have been nothing, but given what had happened yesterday, and the car bomb in the parking lot, he wasn't going to take any chances.

Natalie leaned against the hood of his truck, waiting for him to open the doors.

"Step away from the truck," he said, trying not to sound too overly concerned, but serious enough that she would move.

She pushed off from the truck, looking back at it over her shoulder as she rushed to his side. "What is it? Is something wrong?" Her eyes were wide with fear.

He shrugged. "I'm sure it's nothing, but I

just want to check things out. We don't want another bombing."

She visibly relaxed, her shoulders lowering from her ears. "No one knows we're here. We're good. You can relax," she said, waving him off.

"A person is at the most risk when and where they feel the most comfortable." He tried not to preach, but she needed to make sure she was as committed to her security as he was. "Look there," he said, pointing at the scuff mark on the ground. "You see that?"

She nodded.

"Overseas, that would be a key indicator that someone had been messing with our rigs."

"Thankfully, we are not overseas and, like I said, no one knows we are here. You know, you may want to talk to someone about PTSD. You've obviously been through a lot and one of the key identifiers in recognizing a person has it is that they begin to see threats in ordinary places."

He appreciated that she was worried about his mental health, seriously. There was no doubt in his mind that his life had been impacted by the things he had seen, but there was a thin line between being vigilant and safe, and complacent and dangerous. He would always choose to be aware of his surroundings because even when he was, things like what happened yesterday still had a way of coming around. And so far his vigilance had kept him alive and might help her stay that way, as well.

"Just go with me on this, please," he said, trying to keep his mixed emotions from leaking into his voice. "It's my job to worry about you, and to make sure you are safe."

The lines around her eyes softened and she smiled at him, then motioned toward the truck. "I suppose it doesn't hurt a thing to check and make sure that nothing is amiss." She paused and looked away. "And thank you. I really do want you to know how much I appreciate everything you're doing for me. I will make sure that your company gets paid for your services."

Though he heard everything she had said to him, all he could take from it was that she had relegated him to the level of the help. Had that been a way for her to keep her feelings at bay? Or had she finally just realized that she was too good for him? Either way, she wasn't wrong. He was here to labor for her, nothing more.

He hated that the woman of his dreams was standing at his fingertips, yet a world away.

"Don't worry about paying me. I'm here because I want to be here. This, taking care of people, is who I am." He put his hand to his heart.

And not because he thought she was beautiful. And not because right now, as he looked at her, all he could see was the sparkle of the morning sun in her eyes—and it made them appear even more green than when he had first looked upon her face in Judge Hanes's office.

He would keep her safe because that was what he had been born to do. And if this day was his last day because of this mission in life, at least he had led a life built on purpose and ended on a day in which he had felt her lips.

"I should have known you were the hero type." She smiled and touched his back, the first time she had touched him since they had been in the room alone together. "A girl could fall for that kind of thing, you know."

He half expected her to say, "But I'm a woman" and yet, she said nothing.

Did that mean that she was falling for him, or was that just wishful thinking?

And this, this mind game, this confusion, was what he hated the most about feelings and romantic attachments. It had a way of making a man feel crazy. Did she mean what she was saying or did it mean something else? Was she flirting with him or was he hoping to see something that wasn't really there?

It was so much easier just to stay in the friend zone.

"Let me go check on the truck." He hurried over to the driver's side and dropped down to the ground, hugging it like it was the lifeline that would keep him from falling into the trap that was his feelings.

He closed his eyes and took in a long, deep breath. The earth smelled of decay and dust and the heady aroma of burnt frost. Every place he had ever been in the world had smelled different, but the salty, mineral scent of dust was universal—it whispered of unanswered dreams, lost hopes, failed promises, false starts, spilled blood and the ashes of lives. And yet, behind those whispers were screams of the venerable and lives built on honor and joy. People had called him a hero in the past, but those who experienced the brief periods of time on the earth with love, honor and joy were the most heroic of all.

They had lived lives worth all the hell he put himself through in order to protect them. And he wished that Natalie would have all of those things, even if that future never crossed paths with his—and he gave every one of his days to the task of making her life one she, the hero, deserved.

Her secret protector. Forever.

He dabbed at the chill on the tip of his nose as he moved to inspect the undercarriage of the truck. The area right above his head had been wiped clean of dried mud and debris.

Odd.

There was no way that spot would have been clean given the number of miles they had racked up. Was his mind just playing tricks on him, and he was seeing things that weren't really there? He had been known to do such things—see threats where they weren't—in situations like this before. He stared at the clean spot on the undercarriage, wishing he knew slightly more about cars than what he did. Sure, he was competent, but being a full-blown mechanic wasn't in his wheelhouse.

Then he saw it. There, next to the crossmember, below his driver's seat, was a small black box. Unlike in the movies, there was no blinking red light or something to indicate that power was going to the IED. Instead, it was just a simple black box, and if he hadn't been looking for it or if he hadn't seen the scuff marks underneath the car, there was no chance he would have ever seen the object, even with a quick undercarriage inspection. That was what made these things so goddamn deadly.

He tried to control his breathing as he slipped out from underneath the truck.

Just like that, everything he had been thinking about and all the emotional turmoil he had been putting himself through, all came to a screeching halt. That box. It looked like nothing more than hard plastic put together with four little screws. Whoever had made the bomb must have used a screwdriver normally set aside for glasses and delicate work. Specialty screwdriver. Specialty chemicals. Specialty bomb maker.

At least he wouldn't have died at the hands of just some inept person who had gotten lucky.

And he had saved Natalie. He had trusted his gut, listened to the little voice screaming at him...the little voice he had wanted to ignore... and it had proven effective. To think he had almost let his mind grow clouded with things nonessential for survival. If he was going to protect her, he needed to focus.

He had to tell her what he had found, but he didn't want to alarm her. There were so many things that swept through his mind—how they had been found, who was behind it and what their possible next moves were. And yet, he couldn't find the air to make the words. It was as if the bomb had already gone off in his mind, sucking every syllable into its mushroom cloud and leaving him as nothing more than skin and bones.

"Are you okay?" Natalie asked, staring at

him. "Is something wrong…something with your truck?"

He opened his mouth, then closed it, hoping the air would move back into his lungs and his tongue would work to sound out the words that had to be said. Instead, none came and he wrapped his arm around her shoulders. She didn't hesitate as he led her back to the house and walking inside, making sure to close and lock the front door behind them. Judy must have been in the kitchen. He heard the water running there.

He let go of her, hurrying around the living room and making sure all the curtains were closed. No one could see inside. He couldn't allow them to become even easier targets than they already were.

"What is going on, Evan?" Natalie asked, this time sounding more frantic than she had before.

"I don't want you to get upset." His words sounded out of place even to his own ears.

"I'm well past upset. What in the hell is going on?" Natalie sounded absolutely terrified—the one thing he had wanted to avoid.

"Don't worry. Everything will be fine." He knew she could hear the lies in his sound, regardless of the words he had chosen to try and assuage her terror.

She moved beside him and stepped to the window, but he pushed her back. Her eyes and mouth opened wide, as though he had struck her instead of attempted to protect her.

"I'm sorry, I didn't mean—"

"What in the actual hell—"

"There is another bomb." He spit the words like they themselves were a ticking time bomb.

All the color in her face drained away. From her look, he could tell that the air had left her just as it had left him. He wanted to pull her into his arms and tell her that it would be okay. That this little setback was nothing. That they were safe. That they hadn't been found and that no matter what, nothing would happen to her while he was there.

But he couldn't lie to her.

She had every right to be frightened.

He didn't have to like it. And it made his bones ache in a way he had never thought possible just from looking at another person and empathizing with what they were going through, and yet, here he was.

Judy walked into the living room, drying her hands on an embroidered cheesecloth dish towel that reminded him of his grandmother. The embroidery was green and pink, a little girl in a bonnet and a daisy in her hair.

"I thought you guys were heading out. Did

you change your minds? Forget something?" Judy smiled, but as she looked at Natalie, her smile disappeared.

The delicate towel slipped from her hands and fell to a heap on the floor. She ran to Natalie and wrapped her in her arms just as he had wanted to do. "It's going to be okay."

The steel and stone he had put around his heart started to crack ever so slightly.

"Someone planted a bomb underneath my car."

"When? Now? Last night?" Judy asked, taking over the questioning from Natalie like they were of one mind.

"Mom, it's okay," Natalie said, nodding as she wiggled from her arms. "You don't need to worry about anything. I'm sure it is just a training exercise or something. Isn't that right, Evan?" She gave him a look to play along.

He nodded, but he didn't like this. He'd had enough of the lies and the deceit. It hadn't gotten them anywhere but sleeping in a room alone together—and then falling into one another's arms and making the world more complicated.

"Judge DeSalvo, I think that, given the circumstances, we need to tell your mother the truth." He looked at Judy. Her shoulders fell and there was tiredness in her eyes that he had seen every time he'd ever watched a heart break.

Natalie sighed, giving up on their charade. "You're right, Mr. Spade."

She made his name sound like it was something less-than, but it could have been the resignation that marred her words.

"Mom," Natalie continued, "Mr. Spade was assigned to protect a fellow judge. There has been a series of attacks and we are concerned for my safety. As you can surmise, given the nature of this latest blow, we aren't completely out of the woods. Clearly, someone must still be targeting me."

"Do you know who it is?" Judy answered.

"Not yet, but we are working on tracking down leads."

He had to jump into action, to do something that would make this all okay and ensure their safety. He took out his phone and dialed his team.

A.J. answered. "What the hell is going on?"

"Hey, tool bag, you guys doing okay?" Evan asked, making his way out of the living room and away from the two ladies. No doubt they would need a minute while Natalie filled Judy in on all the details.

"We are holed up on the homestead. All is good. You? Zoey said you had found yourself in a little action yesterday. Shit blow over yet?" A.J. asked.

"No, but that is why I'm calling. We got an IED. I need the team to come out, see what we can do to neutralize the threat." He tapped in the address and sent it to A.J. via text. "And I'm hoping you guys can get me some kind of information from it. Something to narrow down the list of suspects."

He could hear A.J. turn away from the phone and give whomever was in the office with him the order to get everyone pulled together.

A.J. had always gotten such a high from those moments, the rush of the call to action and the thrill of the unknown. It felt so good on that side of the ticket, and a whole hell of a lot better than it did when Evan was the one who had been forced to call in the team. Evan couldn't do this alone, but at the same time it made him feel weak that he had to turn to them. Yet, he didn't know why. This kind of thing, calling for assistance when he needed it, was just another day on the job.

Why did it bother him so much this time?

A.J. came back to the phone. "We will be there within a couple of hours. We'll put together an extraction plan, but for now you need to sit still. We don't want you getting into any type of confrontation with the enemy without your backup in place. Got it?"

His brother, always the man to spring into

Chapter Seven

Another bomb. Another freaking bomb. Before yesterday, Natalie had thought that car bombs were something that only really happened in war-torn nations and action movies. They certainly didn't happen in her mother's driveway in a tiny town in the middle of the woods in Montana. This just didn't make sense.

Until now she had really started to believe that the person behind it was Sanders or Rencher, after talking through that case with Evan last night. But she didn't recall that either of them had ever had this kind of know-how… or had been trained in the administration of nerve agents. Whoever was trying to kill her and Judge Hanes was a highly skilled mercenary…someone just like Evan.

She glanced in the direction of the driveway, where he was now standing with several other people who resembled him. The dark-haired man to his left looked almost identical to him, but was a few years older and had at least three inches on him. They had the same dark, brooding stare and as the man looked toward the house, she noticed that they had the same smoldering gaze when they were deep in thought.

Evan couldn't have been behind anything like this.

Her mind wandered. He had been present for the nerve agent attack, the bombing and the bombing attempt. In court, a lawyer would have argued that his being at all three events was nothing more than coincidence—circumstantial evidence—and there was nothing that directly linked him to the crimes. But what if whomever was coming after her and Judge Hanes was really targeting him?

She nearly laughed out loud at the thought. The idea was outlandish. He had been hired because Judge Hanes had received a threat; he hadn't brought trouble to them. She was just being crazy and trying to find fault where none lay.

Though she wasn't sure which of her actions had brought violence to her doorstep, she wasn't the kind of woman who would shirk accountability. If she had triggered this, then she was the one who needed to take responsibility for it, and then work to make sure it was peacefully resolved. As much as she didn't understand the why, she did understand her duty to herself and the people who had elected her a judge.

And maybe that was exactly what this was—someone's best attempt to keep her and Hanes from doing their job. She had been looking at the last few cases, but she had been foolish not to look ahead.

She wished she had her cell phone so she could pull up her caseload. Regardless, whether she located her enemies or not, they would continue to breathe down her neck. She was at their mercy until they chose to reveal themselves.

What kind of hellish reality had she found herself in?

She thrived on always listening to explanations, having some kind of answer at her beck and call, and then administering judgment with the strike of her gavel. Yet, here she was, stuck in the mire of anonymity and secrets. She could only hope that it wouldn't last much longer.

Whoever was gunning for her would have to step out of obscurity soon. She knew their game; it was a game she had played in a million different ways, and a game she could win.

"Are you okay, honey?" Judy asked, putting her hand on her shoulder and pulling her from her moodiness.

"Yes. You?" She forced a smile. "I feel like I need to apologize. I didn't intend on—"

"We are rarely allowed the ability to have our intentions reflect our reality. I know you did what you thought was best." Judy gave her a light kiss to the cheek, the same action she had used when she was younger and at odds with her soul. Even then, it had helped to calm the raging tempests. "And even if you had brought an entire army to my doorstep, I would still say let them come. You are more important to me than anything. If you need a safe haven, my doors are always open."

She touched Judy's cheek as they stood together watching the war outside her window. "You are far too kind to me. You always have been. I hope you know how grateful I am to have you in my life. Always."

"I could say the same thing to you, my dear." Judy patted her hand and gave it a squeeze. "My life was empty without you in it. You have given me purpose. My only regret is that I don't get to have more time with you. So really, if nothing else, this time together is a gift."

Only Judy could see a fight for life and death as a gift. It was this perspective that made her so special. She was one of those rare people who always saw the world through rose-colored glasses and looked for opportunities in the hardest of days.

"Why are you talking like this?" Judy's eyes darkened with concern. "What is going on? Is there something else you aren't telling me about what's happening here?"

"No," she said, feeling the weight of the word. "I'm sure this will all be taken care of shortly and we will all be safe."

Evan walked toward the door, his eyes even darker than Judy's as he looked in at them. Had he found something else? Some new threat?

She was strong, life had stripped any softness from her, but she wasn't sure how much more she could bear.

She had a gnawing feeling she had just told Judy a lie. Safety was a promise she shouldn't and couldn't make.

Evan made his way inside, and the curl of his shoulders and the heaviness in his steps made her want to tell him to sit down and rest. He wasn't the kind to stop, at least she didn't think so. But what did she really know about this man, this man whom her heart ached for? Maybe the ache was nothing more than some kind of hero worship or Stockholm Syndrome—though the only person who kept her prisoner was herself.

Until now she had prided herself on her independence and strength. However, looking deeper into herself, those qualities were also her weaknesses. They held her in place as much as they pushed her forward.

Would she ever be enough? Or was such a thing even possible?

There were days when *enough* seemed nearly doable, but then things like this happened and the world rained its anger down—not just on her, but everyone who wanted to do something good. Or was *good* also an illusion?

What was the point of all the anger, hate and pain that came with living if good, right and just were only illusions?

"I always hate when people tell me I look tired," Evan started, glancing over at her. "But if you are half as tired as you look—"

She waved him to a stop. "That's just a way of politely telling people that they look like crap, and you don't need to tell me. I feel it." She tried to smile, the simple action some kind of gesture of appeasement in order to help him understand that she wasn't upset with his assessment of her. "From the look on your face, it's clear you have something you don't want to tell me. What is it?"

He glanced down at his hands and then back up at her.

Judy cleared her throat. "I will go put a kettle on for tea. If anyone wants to warm up, you know." She excused herself.

Evan strode over to the couch and sat down on the edge, steepling his fingers between his knees as he attempted to collect himself before speaking. She wanted to tell him to just start talking, to tell her everything that was on his mind and what he had found out, but terror rattled through her. Whatever he was about to tell her was going to be the kind of ugliness that tore a soul apart.

Finally, his gaze found hers. "Did you ever hear about the Unabomber?"

She nodded, her throat tightening with his every syllable.

"Did you ever hear about his bombs, his signature? You know the way the FBI was finally able to tie him to several of his devices?"

She shook her head.

"In every one of his bombs, there was a metal plate—usually in the end of the pipes. He would stamp initials into them—FC. And even though many of these plates were destroyed in the explosion, the FBI's teams were able to reconstruct them."

She didn't know what the Unabomber, Ted Kaczynski, had to do with what she was going through. He was in prison, and definitely not responsible for these bombs.

"The FBI found a metal plate, similar to what the Unabomber used."

"What?" she asked. "Have you been working with the FBI?"

"My team is working with Agent Hart from the Missoula office. He was nice enough to send us a copy of the bomb's parts to see if we could make sense of it." He swallowed hard, making her wonder what else he held back.

No doubt he had more contacts in the Bureau and every other alphabet soup acronym agency from a variety of governments. And here she had assumed, up until now, that she was the one with all the political pull. He could probably work over her head, if he needed to. Hopefully, she would never have to find out if she was right or not.

"Anyhow," he continued, "have you ever heard of Rockwood?"

She did a quick inventory, but couldn't think of anything offhand and she shook her head.

"They are a manufacturing company, one with a desire to be involved in helping to develop weapons for the government. They have been known to do some questionable things in order to try and get their hands on manufacturing contracts, including but not limited to murder and blackmailing international diplomats."

"And you think they have something to do

with the bombing?" she asked, confused how a company she had never heard of would have anything to do with her attempted murder.

Attempted murder. The words made a chill run down her spine.

"We aren't sure if it's just a coincidence or indication of a larger issue, but there has been a recurring issue with Rockwood in and around Missoula County and a variety of businesses that work in that sector. Which leads me to my next question, and while I think I know the answer, I have to ask." He searched her face, but she had no idea what he was talking about.

"What?" she asked, hoping to quell some of the thrashing in her chest.

"Have you had anything to do with any *other* kinds of work, aside from the normal comings and goings of your position as judge?" He didn't blink.

"Are you asking if I have another job…with a *separate* acronym-laden government agency? No." She shook her head vehemently. Working in the CIA or similar agencies would have been a conflict of interest, but she found it a bit of an ego boost that he would think her capable of that.

His lips tightened and he let out a metered breath. "That's not quite what I meant."

And then it hit her. He was asking if she was

on the take, crooked in her dealings. "Evan. You wouldn't." She sat down on the ledge in front of the fireplace at the center of the room. The fire was crackling behind her, but she didn't feel its heat—only the raging fire that swept up from her core at his accusation.

He remained silent. She had expected him to recant, to see what his words had done to her and work to retract them before they had a chance to really burn through her, but he didn't. He simply stood there, watching her. He really was a shadow team man; only those like him could ignore the tension and weight in a room in order to get the answers that they needed. She had thought she'd had the same strength, but she could feel herself charring under his gaze.

"I haven't been a judge for long," she started, but her voice cracked with unwelcome hurt and it forced her to clear her throat. "Even if I had been a judge for decades, I wouldn't act in a way that was less than honorable. I pride myself on my integrity. I wouldn't compromise myself for money."

He nodded, but the power in his eyes remained the same. "Money isn't always the greatest motivator. Many things can make a person act against their character and better judgment if a person is given the right opportunity and motivation."

That was an element of crime she knew all about. And she hated that he thought he could interrogate her like she was on the stand. She could feel the growl forming in her throat, primal and deep. Wolfish.

Silence. Stealth could be one of the greatest assets in a predator's arsenal. This was one of those times in which she needed to bare her teeth, but only when the moment was right.

But it felt wrong that she would look at him this way. He wasn't her prey. He was a fellow predator; an alpha wolf just like her. He had stood at her side and helped her get out of danger, and oh, the way he kissed her lips. If anything, they were the leaders of the pack. They were to stand tall together, not fight amongst themselves.

But he was wrong if he thought he could attack her credibility in any way and not get bit.

"Judge DeSalvo, Natalie." He said her name like it was a whisper on his lips and it made her anger dissipate. "I'm not saying that you have done anything. Know that. All I'm asking is that if you have any *dealings* that I don't know about that could have caused this, it is best if you tell me now. I'm a safe place for you, but I can't help you if I don't know everything."

"You know everything," she said, nearly snarling. "I am not that kind of judge. If you don't believe me, then you can leave right now."

His eyes opened wide. "I'm not leaving you."

"But you don't believe me?"

"Your reaction, that tells me everything I needed to know. Thank you," he said, sounding apologetic but resigned to his method.

"You wanted to make me upset? To get me to a point where I could visualize punching you directly in the nose?"

"Your indignation—it comes from innocence, not fraud," he said, sending her a soft look.

Now she wasn't sure what she was more upset with—him for how he had made her feel or herself for allowing him to emotionally hijack her in this way.

In one of her many classes in college, she had a professor who had spoken on the psychology of crime. She had told the class that to treat feelings as if they were not one of the primary senses—with the same driving needs as hunger or sex—was a mistake. Feelings, in many ways, were often even more of a critical sense than any of the others. They controlled everything, and could be used to control and manipulate a person if they weren't aware.

It wasn't like she didn't face her feelings

every day when she was sitting in the courtroom. She wouldn't be human if she didn't feel hate and disgust when shown many of the things she was required to see. Most of the time she could restrain herself, set her jaw and listen while allowing the time and the lawyers to move forward. She rarely lost her cool, but Evan had broken her down in just a matter of minutes.

What did that mean—was it good that he could make her *feel* when so many others tried and failed, or was it bad for the very same reason?

She sucked in a long breath and exhaled, forcing the questions from her mind. Right now her emotions didn't matter. They had to go back into the little vault at the bottom of her soul where they would remain in perpetuity.

"Now that we have established that I can be trusted, and I hope you can be trusted, what else did you find?" She adjusted the knees of her pants like they were her robe and she was back in her domain.

He furrowed his brows. "In addition to the initials, the FBI sent us the results of their analysis of the chemicals and chemical signatures from the bomb at the courthouse. They want to talk to you, obviously, but we've told them you're in a safe house for now, and you'll be sending a statement."

"Okay, good. I'm glad. Anything of note in the bomb analysis?" Was he going to ask her if she manufactured chemicals and distributed them now, as well? "Did they come from Rockwood's facilities?"

He shook his head. "No, but the chemicals used were odd."

"How so?" She straightened her back.

"I'm sure you are aware, but there are several different classes of fires. Yes?"

She had sat on the bench for a few arson fires, but they had been few and far between and even then, her knowledge of firefighting practices was sparse. "Okay," she said, not sounding overly convincing.

"There are a variety of classes, A, B, C, D and K—all depending on the combustion sources and the requirements needed to combat each type of fire."

She nodded.

"The bomb that this person, or group, placed under your vehicle was created with Class D combustible materials. Meaning they used metals, alkalis to be precise, to create a hot fire that would engulf your entire car."

"So whoever did this not only wanted me

dead, but they wanted to destroy my body, as well?"

His face pinched. "I don't want to jump to that."

Whether he wanted to jump to that or not, it meant something. Someone who perpetuated this level of attack was enraged. They had been pushed to the brink in order to rise to this level of violence and harm. They hated her.

Which meant their attacker either had some sort of mental illness that caused psychosis, or it was likely a person who knew her—and knew her well.

Her chills returned.

"The compounds that they chose to use to create a Class D fire is what got my attention. According to the chemical analysis, the fire was created by using zinc phosphide."

Now he was officially speaking Greek to her. He must have known, based on the look on her face, that she didn't understand.

"It's okay. I had to do a little digging and make a few phone calls to understand, too. Zinc phosphide is used as a rodent killer. Farmers and ranchers kill pests in their fields with it, but few know about its use as a fire catalyst."

She was thankful she had decided to shove her emotions away. She wasn't sure that she could handle all the ramifications that would come with picking apart all the facets of the attack.

"What about the new bomb? Was it made the same way?"

He shrugged. "We are trying to neutralize the bomb, and then my team is going to take it to the Missoula crime lab. I'm not sure if they are going to try and detonate and then analyze or try and work with the bomb as it is. As this attack is the third on a judge, I think they may try to keep the bomb intact."

"I don't want anyone to put themselves in harm's way over this. If we get the choice, I would prefer whoever is working with this does this in the least dangerous way. Can you let them know?"

"I'm sure that they will be safe," he said, walking over to her and putting his hand on her shoulder. "I think it really says something amazing about you that you put the safety of others ahead of the needs of yourself."

She didn't want to blush, but she could feel her cheeks warm. "It just doesn't make sense. We will get this perpetrator one way or another."

His fingers pressed against her, and she wanted to move her body closer to his and lean on him, but she stopped herself.

The windows rattled and she felt the blast

against her skin. She fell to the ground, not sure if it was him pushing her or her pushing him, but they moved together and pressed their bodies low.

She turned her head, looking in the direction of the blast, expecting the windows to be spider webbed with fracture lines, but they were standing as they had been only moments before.

Through the ringing in her ears, there was the din and rise of a man's wail—it sounded almost like a howl. She looked to Evan. Over his right eye was a long, bloody gash. His lips were open and she realized he was the one, the wounded animal, whose call pierced her soul.

Chapter Eight

He sat up, trying to figure out what exactly had happened to him. Evan ran his fingers over his forehead and drew them back; they were covered in blood. He tapped his fingertips together feeling the stickiness, like he hadn't felt it a thousand times before. What had happened to him?

All he could remember was there was a loud blast and then nothing but darkness. And yet, somehow, he had found himself sitting alone in a hospital room, only God knew where.

He pressed the little button at the side of his bed. The bed was hard, unforgiving, as he rolled to his side and he was almost positive he smelled moth balls and mildew, but he wasn't entirely sure. He pressed the call button again, but nothing—no static or ward secretary answered his buzz. But he could see a thin light casting an orange shadow over his door from out in the hall.

He took in a deep breath. Over the scent of his moldy bed, the odor of cleaning products and decay wafted to him. The 1970s orange-and-brown curtains strung up around the bed would have been a dead giveaway that he was in some kind of throwback facility. It kind of reminded him of hospitals in nonindustrialized, poor countries. In fact, quite often third-world countries' hospitals were far better than this; at least there he had been able to watch the flurry of nurses and doctors rushing between rooms.

"Hello?" The eerie silence made him wonder if he wasn't stuck in some sort of purgatory-like dream. He called out again, but there was still no answer.

Was this death?

It wouldn't have surprised him. This would be the type of place he would have been sent to upon dying. He had always expected to die all alone, and find himself sequestered in the one place he hated more than anywhere else.

He swung his feet around to the side of the bed, but as he sat upright his head swam and his vision blurred. Nope, he definitely wasn't dead. If he was, he wouldn't have felt this crappy.

The light stopped flashing in the hall, and a woman stepped into his room. Saying she looked like Nurse Ratched would have been a compliment. The woman standing in front of him was in her late sixties and her lips were creased with the folds of a lifelong smoker. When she saw him, her mouth curled up with disgust and he noticed a scar on the side of her nose, like she had long ago lost in a bar fight.

"What the hell do you think you're doing?" She rushed toward him. "You shouldn't be sitting up. You need to be resting. I thought I told you this before."

The way she talked to him made him wonder if he had woken up once before, but didn't remember it. Was there something very wrong with him? Did he have some sort of short-term memory loss going on, or was it something worse?

"Where am I?" He glanced down at his bloody fingers, and they swirled in and out of focus.

She frowned as she basically pushed him back down onto his bed and fluffed the pillow around his head. "You are at the Marcus Memorial Hospital just outside Silver Mountain. Your friends brought you here after a particularly nasty fall."

He tried to relax into the bed, but as he moved a spring rose up from the mattress, poking him in the back. Really, what kind of hospital was this? If they were trying to legitimize their services and reassure their patients that they were getting the highest-level care possible, they were failing—hard.

"Wipe that look off your face. You are lucky that you have a bed. It's not every day a veterinary hospital finds themselves caring for a two-legged creature. If this hadn't been a hospital decades ago, you wouldn't even have this kind of luxury."

"Wait… I'm in a damned *veterinary* hospital?" He couldn't help the little laugh that escaped his lips at the thought of the situation in which he found himself.

"Yes. And to be clear, I like dogs far better than humans." She walked out of the room, but a second later she looked back in from the hall. "But if you are a good boy, I might have your girlfriend bring you in a dog treat."

"Natalie is here?" he asked, but as he did, he realized she had been the first person he had thought of when the woman said *girlfriend*, even though there were many women friends in his life.

He had promised himself that he wouldn't think of her like that, and yet, after a near-death experience, his instincts had acted and shown him exactly who and what he wanted. Maybe it was just his loneliness rearing its ugly head.

Yep, he was buttoning that crap up.

"She is out in the waiting room." The nurse

didn't say anything and ducked back out of the room.

Was she going to tell Natalie he was awake? Send her in? Who else was there?

He opened his mouth to yell after the woman, who he realized now wasn't actually a nurse but likely a vet tech who had been tasked with babysitting him. No wonder she had been so annoyed. He should have told her he preferred the company of animals, too; maybe it would have softened her up a bit.

He touched his head again, this time letting his fingers rest on the edge of his cut where the blood had started to dry. He couldn't have been here too long if his wound was still weeping. That was something. And his cut mustn't have been too bad if they hadn't treated it while he was unconscious. Maybe it was nothing more than a bad scrape; faces tended to gush. And there was just enough redhead in him that he was more of a bleeder than most people he knew. It was probably his Irish blood.

He tried to catch a glimpse of himself in the window to the left, but all he could see were the snowcapped mountains that were just outside his touch. The mountains were craggy, granite beasts like rock trolls from worlds past who had collapsed in battle and broke apart under the weight of the sky.

A profound sadness filled him, but he didn't know if it was because he felt like one of those trolls himself or if it was just the melancholic grayness of the frozen world. Or maybe what was bothering him was that in his pain, he was alone.

There was the patter of footsteps and he looked in the direction of the sound. Natalie poked her head into the room. "You decent?" She sent him a dazzling smile.

"If you mean dressed, yes." He ran his hand over the leg of his black pants, not caring about the bloody mark it would leave behind.

She walked in carrying the blue-and-white cups that seemed to be in every medical facility in every part of the globe. For a brief moment he wondered why that was. Maybe they were a requirement to be certified for treatment. Or maybe they came free with every order of medical supplies. *Here are your ten boxes of nitrile gloves, and with it one thousand crappy cups. Free!* His thoughts came in a voice reserved for late-night infomercial actors. It made him chuckle.

Maybe the blow to the head had caused more damage than he had initially realized.

She handed him a cup of coffee. It was swirling with cream, and his heart warmed ever so slightly. "You look like I would expect after you took a lamp to the head," she said, grimacing as she stepped closer and looked over his forehead. "I told them to leave the gash alone. They wanted to stitch it up, but stitches leave scars and I didn't know if you were the kind of guy who would be averse to such a thing."

"You think I care about my looks?"

She reached over and gave his beard a little tug. "I don't think that you are indifferent, Grizzly Adams."

"Oh, popping out the old-school movie references today, I see." He touched her hand as she drew away from his beard. "I like it."

It struck him that in this moment, it wasn't the things that were being spoken aloud that were being said. Rather, the real conversation was happening in the ways her eyes looked pained when she gazed at his wound and the tenderness with which her fingers had touched his hair.

She didn't love him, he didn't see that in her, but he could see an affinity.

Here he had been thinking he was all alone, when in fact, he had a friend who was only a few footsteps away and waiting to touch him just like that. She didn't have to love him; that was fine. But he was certainly beginning to have an affinity for her, as well.

As long as they were working together, he would be more than happy to communicate in this unspoken language of touches and looks. If a kiss happened again, he would suffer through it, as well. He smirked. Yes, the only word for kissing her was *suffering*; for to kiss her would be to open his heart, and to open his heart was to open himself up for the pain that came with love. And to love, that was the worst kind of pain of all.

Here was hoping she could keep her emotions in check when she was around him and keep them to only a low-grade crush. She probably had the emotional fortitude of a saint. At least, he'd wish.

He took a sip of the coffee and though she had tried to fix it up for him, it still carried the ashy flavor of cheap grounds. This place really had been a hospital in the last century, and apparently, the coffee was from those days, too.

But he wasn't about to complain; it was still better than the coppery flavor of blood that had settled into the cracks of his lips. He let the cream soak into his tongue.

"Your phone has been buzzing nonstop," she said, handing it over to him. "I haven't looked at anything, but I think you have a lot of people who want to know you are okay. Don't worry. I got in touch with the FBI and let them know what was happening."

"My team here, too? Did anyone else get

hurt?" he asked, looking behind her like they were about to walk in, as well. He clicked on the screen. Natalie was right: twenty missed calls and thirty-six text messages were waiting for him. He clicked off the screen. He'd focus on them when he could muster more brainpower.

She shook her head. "Everyone else walked away unscathed. They are still on the farm. Your brother felt terrible about what happened. He hasn't stopped apologizing and I bet that at least half of the messages on your phone are from him." She gave him a slight smile.

"He should feel bad. Did a lamp actually fall on my head? Is that what hit me?" he asked. "And by the way, thanks for no stitches. I will take some skin glue, though."

She reached into her pocket and drew out a brown antique-looking bottle. She opened it, and with it came the scent of pain. He lost count of the number of times he used that particular crap on his skin. Would he ever get used to that sensation, the burning and ache of the antiseptic glue as it touched the newest scar on his soul?

"Here, I've got it for you," she said. "It's going to hurt."

All that he knew. As a brush touched his forehead he tried not to grimace.

"You're taking this like a champ." She brushed

on a second coat of the glue as she pressed the edges of the wound together. The pinching almost hurt worse than the glue.

"What can I say? I'm a tough guy," he said, a touch of ego flecking his voice.

She chuckled, but he could tell she was trying to bite it back.

"Trying to work here," she said.

"Thanks for doing this. I appreciate you not letting the vet do the heavy lifting here."

She nodded. "Your brother wasn't sure how bad your injuries were, so they did run a series of X-rays on you. Wanted to make sure there was no major internal bleeding. From everything they could find, it seemed like the only injury was to your head. So no major damage." She laughed.

"Oh, I see how it is. As long as my body is okay and ready to function, you're not worried about me," he teased. "I should've known you only liked me for my body and not my brain."

"I said no such thing," she said, smiling wide. "But yeah, I admit it. I'm only after you for your body." She let go of his forehead and he could feel the pull of the dried glue. She slapped his arm as she turned away and slipped the skin glue back into her pocket. "Actually, I was worried about your brain. But until you were awake, there wasn't a whole lot we could do here. There was talk about sending you back to Missoula for more testing, but given the circumstances, I didn't think that was the best idea."

And just like that, he was back to reality. He needed to get back to work. He was the one who was supposed to be protecting her, and yet, she was the one gluing him up and standing over him in his time of need. This was not how it was supposed to go.

"Is your mom okay? Did my team get her out?"

She nodded. "They didn't tell me where they were taking her, but I think it was better that way. If my enemies can't get their hands on me, I don't think that they would go after her, but I don't want to take the risk." She sighed. "My mom's already been through so much and this is all very stressful for her."

"I'm so sorry this happened. I thought I'd cleared our escape of any tails, but it's pretty hard to shrug anybody off in Montana when there's only one main interstate. They must've had people spread out on a few exits and used a team to follow us. It's what I would've done if I was in their shoes. From our perspective, everything would look all right. I put your mom in danger." He realized he was explaining this mostly for his benefit. Maybe it was his attempt to assuage some of the guilt he was feeling over bringing her enemies directly to her most sacred location.

She shrugged. "My mom has always been a fighter. She would be happy to take up arms against whoever is doing this—she already told me. She's a tough cookie, but she's the only family I have left and I don't want to put her in danger. So I'm glad you called in your people."

He nodded, only wishing he had gone to them sooner. "What about you? Are you doing all right?" He looked at her.

"I'd be lying if I said I was fine, but I know we will get through this."

His phone buzzed in his hand and he looked at the screen. A.J. was calling.

"Answer him," she said. "I know he's worried and I haven't had a chance to call him and let him know that you're awake."

He nodded, clicking on the call. "Hello?"

"Holy balls, it's alive!" A.J. sounded positively enthusiastic. "Dude, of all the ways I thought you would go out, a lamp to the head—unless wielded by a woman—was the last thing I thought would happen."

"Wielded by a woman? No, man, that's something that would happen to you."

A.J. laughed. "Well, I'm glad you're feeling better. Asshat. You had us all real worried for you."

"You know, you wouldn't have had to be worried about me if you would have all just handled the explosives with slightly more care. What the hell were you doing, playing football with the car bomb?"

A.J. laughed, but this time the sound was more clipped, anxious and guilty, no doubt. "Hey, you should be thanking me. At least I pulled it off your truck before it detonated."

"I'm surprised. You've been after me to get a truck for a long time. If you blew it up, it would have forced my hand to buy a new one." He laughed. "Was anyone else hurt?"

"You were the only one whose blood was spilled. Truth be told, we think that it may have been on some kind of timer. It was sitting over by the firewood when it went off."

"Good to know that at least our bomber wasn't sitting up in some tree. I was worried it was a remote detonator."

"Thankfully, it wasn't, or who knows how many of us would have gotten hurt. We got lucky, man." A.J. paused, like he was letting the words soak in, though he hardly needed to. "Speaking of getting lucky, we also managed to pull a bit more information about the bomb's materials while we were waiting for you, Sleeping Beauty, to wake up."

"I'll Sleeping Beauty you square in the ass if you don't watch yourself," he grumbled.

A.J. scoffed. "Oh, big talk for a dude who got knocked out cold by a lampshade."

"You are asking for an ass kicking."

"Please just change out of whatever little hospital gown they got you all wrapped up in. I don't want you coming after me with your ass hanging out any more than it already is."

He laughed at the mental image. "Ass."

"Jerk."

Goodness, he loved having brothers sometimes. No, make that all *the time.*

"So you got lucky?" Evan asked.

"Yeah, according to the analyst who ran the chemicals, the compound that was used as the bomb's catalyst was a specific kind of rodent bait. It's only sold at three locations in this state and all of them are for industrial uses only. As such, most are sold in bulk and only to professional organizations and industries. Zoey ran through their sales records for the last year. I'll email you what she found. Maybe you can make sense of it."

"Great. And did you get any leads on the pen? The sarin?"

A.J. sighed. "Nothing there, but that is a

chemical that can't be easily made. I'm thinking you got a chemist on your hands—or somebody pretty well trained in chemicals."

"Huh. Damn." He sighed. "Thanks, bro."

"Let me know what you come up with, if anything. Later." A.J. hung up.

A few seconds later his phone pinged with an email of the findings. He opened it up. He scanned down the list of buyers. Many were exterminators and large corporations, but near the middle he found a name that popped. Rencher, and she was listing a textile company in Missoula as the business. A company that worked with a variety of chemicals—and Rencher, working there, must have been well versed in what they could be used for.

But before he could jump to conclusions, he had to make sure of a few things. "Where does Rencher work?" he asked, looking to Natalie.

She shrugged. "All I know was that she owned a textile company in the city. It was one of the main sources of contention in her divorce with Sanders, aside from her kids."

He pushed his legs over the side of the bed. His head was still swimming, but he felt slightly better. Even if he wasn't, there was no sense in staying put. They needed to question their lead suspect.

Chapter Nine

There was no way she was going to let him drive and, though he seemed to understand, he'd been sulking ever since. He had done nothing but stare blankly out the window since they left. Actually, he'd been acting off ever since they'd kissed.

That had been stupid.

It was always a mistake to take any relationship past the point of respectful acquaintances. Beyond that, and she opened herself up to all the reciprocal allowances and allocations required in relationships. It was best to keep the circle small when it came to friends and lovers.

But there was no putting that cat back in the bag. She had given up the truth, that she was attracted to him and wanted him for more than just the protection he provided.

They sat in silence until they were entering the canyon that opened up into the valley and the city at its heart. His eyes darkened as they approached the traffic.

"I hope you don't really mind that I'm driving. If you do, then I think we may need to re-negotiate the nature of our relationship. I don't want a man in my life who is going to be upset when a woman takes the lead." She tried to check herself before she snarled. Even as she spoke, though, she realized that she wasn't really mad at him or mad at all. If anything, she could feel herself grasping at anything that could be used to push him away.

"Huh? What?" He gave her the most confused dude look ever. "What are you talking about? You think I'm mad I'm not driving?"

She huffed. "You've been pouting ever since you got in the car."

He frowned. "One, I'm not pouting. Two, I wouldn't want to drive—you had to help me to the truck. We should definitely not let the dude with a probable concussion drive."

"Then what is wrong with you? Why aren't you talking to me?"

He looked at her and sent her a gentle smile, then reached over and opened his hand and motioned for her to take it. "Natalie."

She stared at his fingers for a long moment. It would feel so good to touch him again, to feel the strength of his fingers against the back of her hand. But was that the smartest thing? She was doing well, or at least she had *thought* she was doing well, in pushing him away.

Reaching over, she took hold of his hand and he wrapped her hand in his. "I didn't even realize I was being quiet. I'm sorry." He lifted her hand and pressed the back of it against his cheek. He was so warm, almost abnormally hot. Why did men always run warmer than women?

"What were you thinking about?" she asked.

He put their entwined hands back down on the console between them. "To be honest, I was thinking how annoying it is to be in an area where my internet doesn't work. It would be nice to be a little more prepared walking into our interrogation."

She nodded. "Do you even think she will be somewhere we can find her?"

He shrugged. "Whoever planted the bomb didn't stick around, at least so far as we could tell. It was more of a drop and trot kind of thing. If she's smart, she will be at work. It would give her a credible alibi."

At least it would be an alibi for today and this morning. But it wasn't that far of a drive to and from the farm and she could have easily made it back and forth in time to get to work.

"Did you look into her phone records yet?"

He shook his head. "My team is supposed to

be doing it, but again, no network." He lifted his phone from where he'd had it perched on his thigh.

They drove out of the canyon and the city was abuzz with midday traffic. The on-ramps were backed up and she pulled behind the long line of cars just as Evan's phone beeped.

"Yes! And we are back online." He tapped away on his device. He rattled off the textile company's address and something about what they did—laundry for local businesses and a few other things—but she was only paying half attention as she drove. "Anyhow," he continued, "it looks like—according to the cell phone tower records—her phone has been in the valley all week and she hasn't gotten any phone calls aside from political spammers in the past sixteen hours."

"That doesn't mean she didn't leave the city limits. It just means she was smart enough to leave her phone at home." It was always the most prolific criminals who knew how to avoid being detected and thus, from being prosecuted.

There was nothing like looking down from the bench, knowing in her gut that the person in front of her was guilty of not only the crimes they were arrested for but also likely a medley of others, and not being able to do a damned thing about it. Instead of saying, "You are free to go," she often wanted to scream.

"As this is our primary suspect, I don't think it's a good idea that you go inside. She may respond better if I questioned her alone."

Natalie bristled. He wasn't wrong, but she didn't want to be left out of the action. "You know, if she is the person we're after, she is going to know exactly who I am, and I'm sure she will make her feelings known. And, if she doesn't recognize me, well…that can be a helpful sign, too."

He sighed. "I should have known you would balk at the idea of not being involved." He gave her hand a reassuring squeeze. "I get it, though. I would be the same way if someone was trying to kill me. Plus, I think it's best if we stick close to one another until we have our suspect in custody."

And there she had been thinking she was going to have to make a stronger argument for not being left in the truck.

"Agreed." She pulled the vehicle to a stop just across the street from the downtown headquarters for the textile company.

The company's front bay doors opened and a large white delivery van made its way out on to the main road. The place was busy as men and women, workers mostly, came and went from the main entrance.

As she watched, she realized she didn't even know the face of the woman they were going to go and talk to. It was dumbfounding. How could this woman want to kill her when she herself didn't even know her face from a million others?

She understood hate; she had felt it countless times just in the past year. And she had long ago realized she could empathize to the best of her abilities and sometimes still not understand what drove a person to do the things they did. In fact, the more time she spent around the public, the less she understood about human nature. There were core needs that never wavered, but how people acquired, kept and maintained those needs were all up for grabs.

"I would say that it may be best for me to lead the questioning when we get in there, but you are pretty unique. You may have more practice in eliciting information than myself. So I guess we will play it by ear. Okay?"

She gave a stiff nod. "And what if this comes to nothing?"

He shrugged. "We will cross that bridge when we get there. Let's just hope that this is our perpetrator and we can get you back to your normal life as quickly and safely as possible."

Did that mean he wanted her gone? No doubt it would be easier for him without her in his life. He could go back to whatever his normal life looked like—a life she had no idea about. The realization made her ache. She couldn't make him open up to her any more than he naturally did, but that didn't mean she didn't want him to.

He gave the back of her hand a quick kiss before letting go and getting out of the truck. He walked around to her side and opened the door for her. The simple act of chivalry surprised her in all the right ways. It had been a long time since a man had gone out of his way to do anything for her, unless it was in the courtroom—where everyone was always trying to buy her favor.

He helped her out. His walk was steady; he must have been feeling better. She wanted to ask him if he was feeling okay and if he was really up for doing this, but even if he wasn't, she was positive he would lie to her in order to get the job done…and get her out of his life, maybe.

Then again, he had been so kind to her and held her hand.

He opened the door for her and followed her inside; meanwhile, she reminded herself that just because a man was kind didn't mean that he was flirting with her.

The man at the front counter looked up from his phone and barely masked his disgust at having been disturbed. "Help ya?" he asked, his words truncated, like it took too much effort to say a complete sentence.

She disliked him already.

"We are here to see Ms. Rencher or Ms. Sanders, if one of them is available." As Evan spoke, the man smirked like he knew a secret they weren't privy to...a secret he was dying to tell.

"Ms. Rencher is in the back. She doesn't like being disturbed these days." The man looked back and forth between them, seeming to hint at the divorce to see what they knew.

She made sure to keep her expression as neutral as possible. This young, disgruntled man couldn't know she was one step from running away, that a lump had formed in her throat that threatened to strangle her from the inside out, or that the last thing she wanted to do was look her potential murderer right in the eyes.

She could only imagine how it would feel to see such unbridled hate directed solely at her. What if the woman was carrying a gun? She could draw and fire before Natalie even knew she was under threat. Sure, they were in public, but that likely wouldn't stop this killer.

Her hands started to sweat.

Until now she hadn't thought about the feelings that were enveloping her and threatening to unleash a panic attack.

At least she wasn't facing this alone. Or, worse, having to sit idly by while others handled the entire situation. At least by taking an active role in bringing down her assailant, she held control over her own welfare.

The man picked up the phone, said a few quick words and turned back to them. "She said she'll be right out. Good luck."

Her heart raced, and she tried to take back control of herself by counting her breaths. One. Two. Three.

The door leading to the back opened, and a brunette woman stepped into the lobby. Her hair was loose, cascading down her shoulders, and she was far younger than Natalie had assumed she would be. If she had to guess, she was somewhere in her midthirties. When the woman saw her, she sent her a big smile.

Was it fake? Was she pretending she didn't know her?

"Hi, how can I help you guys?" Ms. Rencher asked, her voice high and chipper.

The man who had greeted them in the lobby had warned that she was not one to be trifled with, and yet, this woman was nothing like she had expected. It had to be a show.

"If you wouldn't mind excusing us," Evan said to the other man, who was now standing and watching them with a bemused look on his face.

The man dipped his head in acknowledgment before making his way out. She couldn't help but notice that he looked over his shoulder one more time before letting the door slip closed with a click.

The woman frowned. "What is going on here?"

Evan smiled, but even someone who didn't know him would have known that the action was false. "We are here thanks to an investigation in a case of attempted murder." He paused.

The woman cocked her head to the side, looking confused. "I don't know how I could possibly be able to assist you with anything to do with murder."

The woman's gaze never moved to Natalie as she'd have assumed it would have, had Rencher known what Evan was actually talking about. It was strange how the body would give away so many clues, if a person just knew how to watch for them. And Natalie desperately wanted to see something that would prove this woman was responsible for what had happened to her, but right now she wasn't sure if she was actually the person they were looking for.

"I'm certain that is probably the case," Evan said. "However, we just need to make sure we cover all of our bases and talk to anybody that would potentially know anything about the case we're trying to solve."

"Did my ex send you here?" Ms. Rencher's lips puckered and her expression soured. "If she did, you need to know that she is just a vindictive brat. There is nothing she wouldn't do just to screw with me. I can't believe it. And people wonder why I hate her. It's not that I want to hate her. It's just that she keeps doing this kind of crap." She let out a long, tired sigh.

Evan slipped Natalie a look, like he was beginning to think perhaps this woman wasn't who they were after.

"Can you tell us a little bit more about your relationship with your ex?" Natalie asked.

The woman crossed her arms over her chest like she was protecting her core. "We are going through a pretty nasty divorce. Things are getting really heated. And we share a daughter. She is contesting the parenting plan and pretty much everything else. It wouldn't surprise me if she did something like this, and somehow got me involved in a legal battle with potential felonies in order to take away my daughter."

The way she spoke made Natalie wonder exactly what had befallen the woman before they had arrived. Though she had looked through some of her case file, there had been no reference to any crimes beyond the so-called knife fight. Was it possible that the other woman, Ms. Sanders, was responsible for the attacks and was trying to pin it on her ex?

"Do you mind telling me where you were last night?" Evan asked.

The woman shrugged, seemingly unconcerned. "I was here until midnight or so, then I went home."

"Is there anyone who can vouch for your whereabouts for the past twenty-four hours?" Evan asked.

"There was no one here when I left last night, but there are cameras everywhere. And you can definitely take a peek if you'd like. And there's also the camera on my front porch that would show me coming and going last night and this morning."

Evan nodded. He reached into his pocket and withdrew a business card. He handed it over to her. After taking it, she slipped it into her back pocket.

"If you wouldn't mind sending me a digital copy of those videos, I'd appreciate it." Evan smiled. "And hey, if you hear anything that you think would be helpful, don't be afraid to call."

"I just have one more question," Natalie said,

interrupting. "Have you ordered any rodent killer for the business lately?"

The woman pursed her lips, thinking. "We don't have a rodent problem here, so long as I know about. And I definitely haven't ordered anything to mitigate it. Why?"

"Would your ex have access to any of your ordering or business affairs?" Evan asked.

"Unfortunately, yes. I have been trying to remove her from my business accounts, but it is impossible until the final divorce decree is granted. For now she is on most things—even my car insurance," Ms. Rencher said.

"I know just how hard going through a divorce can be," Evan said, ever the kind man she had come to know. "I'm so sorry you are going through this."

The woman looked down at her hands and she could tell that she was struggling in her attempt not to cry.

"I just don't understand why it has to be so hard. What's worse is that we still really do love each other."

Love and hate were sometimes only millimeters apart, and damn if this wasn't one of those times. The poor woman.

"I know this is hard, but we really do appreciate your help." Evan took his phone out of his pocket and pulled up the information his team had sent. "Here is a copy of the rodent killer company's orders for the past few months. Do any of them look familiar?" He pointed at the screen.

The woman squinted like she was having a hard time seeing the type, even though she was relatively young. Oh, had she actually thought *relatively*? Natalie grimaced. The woman was maybe a few years older than she was. Though Natalie felt like a grown adult, big job and all, she wasn't ready to check the box for middle-aged. Not yet anyway.

"Yeah, I didn't make an order, but I can see how you would assume I had. If you like, I'd be happy to show you around the entire facility so you can see that there's nothing like that currently in our possession." The woman seemed genuinely open to their searching the building.

Yeah, this wasn't their person. However, she had a sinking feeling that somehow, she was connected.

The woman squinted harder, pulling the phone closer. "I have to say, though, this guy here, VanBuren, I'm surprised he would make this kind of order." The woman tapped on the screen.

"Why is that?" Evan asked.

"VanBuren is the training officer for the city fire department. He seems like the last person who would order something from this kind of company. He doesn't do any kind of maintenance work for the city, so I can't see why he would need rodent killer." The woman frowned.

The knot in Natalie's stomach tightened. It was odd that a firefighter would need something like this. That was, unless they were going to use it for some kind of training—or he had some kind of vendetta against the district court judges. A city employee, one who worked around criminals and arsonists, could probably name at least one time when they didn't agree with something a judge did. Or maybe the training officer just didn't like them on principle.

Until now the training officer hadn't even crossed their suspects list. However, he did have the knowledge and the access to the chemicals it would have taken to perpetrate the attacks—he may have even had the access to their chambers and to police scanners and informational systems. He could totally be their guy, or not.

If nothing else, they would need to talk to the training officer. Even if he wasn't their perpetrator, he would likely have a wealth of information about who would have access to the knowledge to create the devices that they had found.

Chapter Ten

He was sure that if they went over to Ms. Sanders's that they would run into the same nonanswers that they got from Ms. Rencher. Handling questioning was not one of his favorite exercises. Elicitation had always been Mike's stronger suit. His brother could get answers from just about anyone about anything and his ability to read people was on point. As hard as Evan tried, he had not come by those skills naturally.

Maybe he should call him and have him step in on this investigation. The last he had heard, Troy and Mike were taking turns sitting with Judge Hanes in the ICU.

Thinking about the judge, he took out his cell phone when he got to the truck and typed out a text message to Elle, asking about the judge's status. A few seconds later his phone pinged. Apparently, Judge Hanes was still unconscious, but the doctors were saying he would likely survive.

He asked if they had found evidence of sarin gas.

The lab tests had been inconclusive.

Such a thing wasn't a huge surprise. In the middle of Montana the last thing the doctors would be looking for would be chemical nerve agents. But not knowing what had poisoned Hanes meant lots of dead ends awaited them.

"You okay?" Natalie asked.

He nodded, slipping his phone into his pocket. "Yeah, I'm good. Your friend, the judge, is still alive."

She sucked in a long breath and her hands balled into tight fists.

"I don't have much more information than that. But at least it's something. I'm so sorry, Natalie."

"You've nothing to apologize for. If it wasn't for you, he wouldn't even be alive right now. As it was, he was lucky." Her eyes softened as she looked at him.

"Do you want to see him?" he asked.

She shook her head. "I wouldn't want him to see me like that, so I can't imagine he would want me to see him in that state, either."

He didn't bother to argue. When a power-house was taken out at their knees, they often didn't wish to be seen. The judge likely had enough people coming and going that he wasn't alone.

"The best thing we can do for him," Natalie said, "is to find whoever did this."

He nodded.

"Are you still thinking that whoever poisoned him is likely the same person that planted these bombs? I'm having such a hard time believing that one person could be behind all of this. Poisoning and bombing are so different."

"Are they? If someone is good with chemicals, it really isn't that big of a leap." Evan watched as she started the truck. "Now, we can't be one hundred percent sure this is the same perpetrator, but given the proximity of the events and their rapid succession, if it wasn't the same person, it was at least the same team."

"Do you think it could be one of the divorcées?"

"I think they have a thin motive, but right now they are definitely still on our list. However, I'm not about to stop looking into our other leads."

"I agree. Let's keep this simple." She chuckled. "Let's just keep checking things off and working down our list. Next up, I think we need to hit up the ex, Ms. Sanders."

He nodded, glad to be working instead of

stuck in the heaviness of confusing feelings that had been resting between them.

"Also, about what happened at Judy's…" she started, stripping away any relaxation he was feeling.

"We don't have to talk about that. Let's just call it a lapse in judgment," he said, though he could sense the falseness of his words square in his chest.

From the tired look on her face, she could hear it, as well. "No. We are both adults. We don't get to just sweep what happened under the rug. That's not how it works."

In his experience, that was exactly how it had worked. Then, his previous relationships had been with a different caliber of women. He wasn't used to a woman who pushed for more. If anything, he seemed to attract a certain type of woman, the kind who was looking for danger, a one-night stand that they could tell their friends about, but then never have to worry about calling him again.

He wasn't the kind of man women went to in order to pour their emotions or feelings out, and they certainly didn't expect it of him. The few who had attempted to have a real relationship with him, even his ex-wife, always ended up resenting him for his lack of emotional depth—a problem he really wasn't having with Natalie, which was what confused him the most.

There was something wrong with him; he was aware. Until meeting Natalie, he thought he wasn't like most people in the sense that he didn't want to talk about what he was feeling. He'd never wanted to delve into the deep emotions that came with the relationship or even a real friendship. It was hard enough working with his family. The only thing that kept them strong was the fact that they all had a similar mentality of live and let live.

"So…" she started. "Do you want to treat it like it was a lapse in judgment? Or should we be completely honest with one another? Truth be told, I think you are as lonely as I am."

He was shocked by her candor. He wanted to have some romantic, sweet comeback, but he didn't know what to say. Yes, he was lonely, but that wasn't his driving force for falling for her. But more than anything, he wasn't used to a woman being so open about this kind of thing. It was shockingly refreshing.

He opened his mouth and closed it a few times, hoping that the right words would just come to him. They didn't.

"I'm going to take that as a no." She rounded a corner with the truck. "I know a woman doesn't normally admit that, but I'm not going to play games. And I'm not looking for a one-and-done kind of thing. If I only wanted sex, I would go get sex. It's not hard for a woman to find a lover. That's not what I want. And I know that with everything happening, and with my life hanging in the balance, it isn't the right time for you and me. I do. We need to be focused. But I can't help the way I feel about you. I want more."

To say he was overwhelmed by her openness was an understatement. In many ways, in fact, in all the ways, she was exactly the woman he wanted in his life. But—there was always a but—it *was* the wrong time.

"Do you believe in destiny?" As he asked, he felt ridiculous. "I don't mean like stars in the astrology woo-woo way. I just mean do you think that we are put in place where we are meant to be at certain times?"

As she drove, she nibbled the side of her cheek. "The girl in me says yes, but the judge in me… Well, I just can't say I agree. So many things happen to good people, just because they're in the wrong place at the wrong time. And then they find themselves in front of me. Half the people don't deserve it, or at least they don't seem like they deserve to have been beaten down by life in the ways that they are. If there's something pulling the strings, or call it destiny, or whatever, it's a fickle beast. It's easier to just believe that the world is a random conglomeration of chaos. Sometimes things work out, and sometimes they don't."

"Nihilism from a judge. I should've expected." He sent her his best half grin. "Regardless, I agree with you. It's hard to know exactly what life is really about. However, when it comes to relationships and love, I think that if they're meant to be, they should come to you easily." He shrugged, knowing that what he said was not quite exactly what he meant, but he just couldn't find the right words. Eloquence and discussing emotional matters, well, they weren't his strong suit.

"You think love is easy? That relationships are?" She scoffed. "I thought you said you had been divorced. Regardless, I'd venture to guess that you haven't had many serious relationships. For me, relationships and love are the hardest things not only to find, but also to keep."

Though her words could have been embittered, they weren't. Rather, they sat flat in the air, a simple statement of how he and Natalie differed.

"I suppose you're not wrong. And yeah, I'm not much of a relationship guy. In my line of work, one thing does not lead to the other."

"What do you mean by that?" she asked.

"I just mean that relationships don't lead to happy endings. And working in military contracting doesn't often lead to love—"

"It only leads to death," she interrupted.

At first, her response made him indignant, but then he realized he couldn't really argue. She was right. More, his work led to resentment and hate. And once a person hated something with every fiber of their being, it was hard to even believe that love existed.

Yet, as he looked at her, he couldn't deny love's existence. He would give up his life for her. He would give up everything for her. But he would never ask the same of her; she was far too good for him. If she gave him her heart, it would only break her.

He would be left to live with the weight of the ghost of her love for the rest of his life. Each day he would have to look himself in the mirror and know that he had done a major disservice to a wonderful woman. It was better to call it off now. To stop her from getting any more feelings. If anything, it was the merciful thing to do. It was wrong to make her suffer because of his failings.

"Turn left up here," he said, leading them toward Ms. Sanders's house, according to his records. If she really lived there or didn't, well, they would find out. More than likely, even if she did reside there, she wasn't going to be home in the middle of the day. He should have asked Ms. Rencher more questions.

Though Ms. Rencher had been forthcoming with information, he had learned long ago that the right answers weren't always the most truthful ones.

Natalie followed his directions and the midday sun was high overhead when they finally arrived at a large colonial-style house. Although the paint on its black shutters and white siding had started to crack and peel, it was still beautiful.

After pulling into the driveway, she stopped the truck and they got out. "What if we are too late?" Natalie asked.

"I don't think you can ever be on time when it comes to this type of thing. Chaos, remember?" He sent her a rakish smile.

She laughed, the bright sound breaking through the odd silence that seemed to surround the house and ooze into the neighborhood. She clamped her hands over her mouth, as if she knew how out of place her mirth was.

"Let's just see what we can make of this. What shall be, shall be," he continued.

She reached toward him like she wanted to take his hand, as if they were ascending the walk that led to a weekend dinner party instead of an interrogation. He chuckled as he realized that the difference between the two events was minimal; both were terribly uncomfortable and filled with awkward, deafening silences.

Come to think of it, he preferred interrogation.

Yep, he was definitely some kind of broken.

He knocked on the door, looking around for cameras and surveillance equipment, but finding none. If this was their lead suspect, he had a sinking feeling that they were chasing a dead lead.

He could hear a series of footsteps approaching the door and the slide and click as someone opened a peephole and must have looked out at them. Instead of the door swinging open as he would have expected, the person on the other side stood still as if they were all playing some kind of game of chicken—who would be the first to admit that they all knew what was truly happening?

He was more than happy to take the loss. "Will you please open the door?" He used his deepest baritone, the one he reserved only for moments when he meant business—he called it his "cop voice."

A woman cleared her throat. If he had to guess, she was smoothing herself and trying to shake off any anxiety she was feeling. She'd probably answer the door with a plastic smile.

The door cracked open and a raven-haired woman with deep-set eyes looked out at them. She smiled, but the action was limited to her lips alone. "I'm sorry, I'm not interested." She moved to close the door again, but he pushed his foot into the jamb, blocking her.

"Ma'am, we are here looking for Ms. Sanders. Is she home?" Natalie asked, sounding abnormally breezy and alight with joy.

What were they doing here, playing good cop-bad cop?

He checked himself before he smirked. At least this was better than chicken.

The woman frowned. "She doesn't live here. Actually, she rented this place to me for the next year. She's me and my boyfriend's landlord."

He felt himself relax. "Do you know where we could find her?"

She let the door swing farther open and she turned around like she was going to get something. "Hold on. Let me just see what I have as far as her address. I just send her a check once a month. In fact, we've only lived here about two months." The woman waved behind her like what she was saying was of no consequence.

And maybe to her it wasn't, but to them it could mean a great deal.

"Where you from?" Evan asked.

"Small town on the east side of the state. I just moved over here to be closer to my boyfriend. He needed my help with a few things. Plus, my sister is here in town. Family, ya know?"

Evan nodded. That was nice, but it was a big step for a woman to move for a man. She must have really loved the guy.

"To be honest, I'm not even sure that she's getting these checks," the woman continued. "She hasn't cashed last month's and I sent it two weeks ago." The woman walked back, carrying her cell phone. "I called her to make sure she had received it. I'm a huge fan of direct deposit, but she didn't want to set things up that way. When I called her about the check, she didn't answer. She hasn't gotten back to me."

"Is that normal for her, to be unresponsive?" Natalie asked.

The door opened fully as the woman leaned against the doorjamb and skimmed through her phone. "Like I said, we haven't known each other that long, so I don't really know if that's normal for her. But when I called about renting the place, I got a return call within twenty-four hours. And I was in by the end of the week. She is going through a divorce and it's not going particularly well. I don't know all the details, and I don't press."

He wouldn't press anyone for divorce details, either; to do so was to open a whole floodgate of things he didn't want to talk about. That was one part of life he never wanted to revisit, and if he could have bottled it up and thrown it all away, he would've.

"Here it is," the woman said, lifting her phone so she could show them the contact card for Sophia Sanders. He took a quick photo of it and stuffed his phone back into his pocket.

"Thank you. That will be very helpful. He reached in his chest pocket and pulled out a business card and handed it to the woman. If you hear from Ms. Sanders or you manage to make contact with her in any way, would you please give me a call?" His business card had nothing but his name and phone number, no identifying details. It was so much easier that way.

The lady looked him up and down, staring at the cut on his head for a long moment before letting her gaze move lower and rest on his official-looking suit. "You mind me asking what this is all about?"

Once again, he almost found himself laughing. The regular public could give up so much

information about their life without even realizing it. It struck him right now how easy it
would be to be a criminal. All a person had to
do was appear normal and they could get all
the information they needed from a trusting
person. He wished he could be as obliviously
happy and like the general public instead of
always looking around the corner for the next
possible threat.

"We're just here with her book group." Natalie smiled, and he was impressed with how
quickly she had come up with a lie. "We've
just been worried about her. She hasn't been
attending any of our meetings lately."

"Oh, okay." The woman nodded, seeming
to buy in to the explanation. "I'm a little surprised, though. She didn't seem like the book-
worm type of person."

Natalie's smile widened. "Our doors are open
to anyone who is seeking guidance through
great literature."

Evan took hold of Natalie's hand. "If you're
ever interested," he said, tipping his head in
the direction of the business card in the woman's grip, "you know where to find us. Have a
good day now."

"You, as well," the woman said. "I'll give
you a call, if need requires."

With a backward wave, they retreated. As

soon as they reached the car and got inside, he sighed. "You know, Natalie, you wouldn't make a bad spy."

Chapter Eleven

Natalie was starving. After grabbing a cup of coffee and a muffin to go, they found themselves back on the road. Moving as much as they did, and concentrating on the investigation, she found that she wasn't looking over her shoulder quite as much as she had been when they had been sitting still. People may have been following them, but at least they weren't going to give them enough time to plant another bomb. If they wanted her dead, they would have to physically pull the trigger.

The thought reminded her that maybe she wasn't the most normal person after all. Few people had a preferred method to go in case they were murdered. Given the circumstances, this was the best way she could think of to deal with the pressures around her. She could bury her head in the sand and pretend like her life was filled with roses, but that was so far from the truth. It was better to face things head-on, face the reality presented to her, and deal with it. She'd never be passive.

Perhaps her strength lay in that inability to address life in a laissez-faire fashion. It was remarkably hard to swallow the bitter morsels life shoved down a person's throat; many would've closed their mouths and clenched their jaws tight, then hid away from reality. But not her.

"You feeling better?" She looked at Evan and the puckered, glued gash over his eye. The edges had taken on a dark red color, and a bruise had settled in.

"Huh?" he asked, clearly not following her train of thought. "I'm fine, why?"

"I'm talking about your head. How are you feeling?"

He ran his fingers over the lump on his forehead, stopping at a point that must have been sensitive. "Oh, yeah. I forgot about it. I guess that's a good sign."

"I don't know," she teased. "I think if you start forgetting things, that's actually a bad sign." She smiled.

"I don't know about that. Always found when I start forgetting things, I start feeling better. Maybe it's a bad sign, but it makes for an easier life."

She mulled over his statement. It sat in the air between them for a long moment. She couldn't argue with him. He did have a point. If only she could forget more of the things that happened to her. And once they were through this, she looked forward to being somewhere in the future where she would be able to put this behind her, as well. She'd be fine if it was left to the recesses of her mind, only popping up on occasion, and just as quickly shoved back.

Except that would also mean she would forget about him. That, she didn't want. He had made it clear he wasn't interested in a relationship with her, but he cited time, not the absence of feelings.

If anything, she should've probably been thanking him.

One of them needed to be the reasonable one. They really hadn't known each other that long. And for all she knew he was terribly broken. Men in his line of work typically were. They'd been through so much and seen so much that either they valued love in such an incredible way that they were the greatest of spouses or lovers, or they were the kind that only truly lived for themselves.

From what she could make of it, she assumed it was because they had learned to trust only themselves. And she could understand that. In life and death, people always promised to protect the people they loved and cared about:

their spouse, their lovers, their teammates, their children. But when faced with such realities, those people normally ended up standing alone and completely vulnerable. It was better not to have a connection—he would never let anyone down.

"Do I dare ask what that look on your face is about?" he asked.

Of course, he would be reading her right now, when she had thought she had a good poker face, but he had her rethinking that assessment.

For a moment she considered what she should say in response. To tell him the truth would open up a whole line of conversation that she wasn't certain she wanted to have. Especially given how poorly she assumed it would go—if she brought up the fact that she cared for him, and that she had feelings toward him, no doubt he would once again try to push her away.

But clearly, he could read her face. She was at an impasse. And she sat in silence for a moment too long.

"I retract my question," he said.

She laughed. "Thank you, Counselor."

He shook his head in acknowledgment and gave her a big, toothy grin. In the center of his front teeth was a poppy seed from his muffin. It was exactly what she needed to see in him, some kind of flaw and silly thing to remind her how human and beautifully imperfect he was.

"You have something, right here," she said, pointing to the gap in her front teeth.

"Oh, son of a… And there I was, trying to be cool and stuff," he said, pulling down the visor and opening the mirror behind it. He sucked his teeth before flipping out the debris.

And stuff? Did that mean he was trying to be cute? Did he want her to keep being attracted to him? That he was just as much at odds with his feelings as she was?

Ugh. She couldn't go there. Not now.

"Well, why don't you be cool and tell me how to get to Ms. Sanders's place?"

He quirked an eyebrow, as if he was a bit surprised that she wouldn't fall for his boyish charms. Closing the visor, he opened his phone and rattled off the directions. It wasn't too far from where they found themselves, yet, nothing in the city was more than thirty minutes away on good traffic days.

Today wasn't one of those days. She tried not to lose her patience as she stared out at the jammed mess of cars that sat virtually parked on the road in front of them. For a moderately small city, she would never understand why they had the traffic issues they did. Far larger cities, with less available public transit systems, had them by leaps and bounds when it came to safety and transit times.

She ground her teeth, feeling the muscles in her jaw tense.

"Don't worry," he said, giving her that same smile once more. "Again, manageable chaos. That's all we can hope for in all of this."

"I should have mentioned that in my world, I don't thrive on chaos. I like everything well-ordered and scheduled in advance, at least as much as possible." She tapped her fingers on the wheel. "You should see my house. Everything has its place."

"Ah, you're one of those." He sounded blasé.

"Don't be dismissive of my system. It works for me. Has worked for years now." She smiled, trying to pull him back from judging her too harshly for her near-compulsion. "Don't judge."

"I know…that's your job," he joked. "But tell me, how do you keep your towels?"

"Which ones? Hand, kitchen or bath towels?"

He laughed. "The fact you have to ask me that question tells me most of what I need to know about you."

"What is that? That I'm not a dude who uses one towel for all of his needs?" She smirked. "Remind me to never take a shower at your place—I don't want to get pregnant when I go to dry off."

His mouth opened into an o-shape then he started to give a deep belly laugh. "Of all the things I thought you would say, that was the last thing I imagined coming out of your mouth," he said between bouts of laughs. "But I have to admit. I kind of like all the places your mind went right there. Most of all, you thinking about taking a shower at my place."

She wasn't sure that he really meant that; most men would've gone the other direction with where her thoughts had gone.

"By all means, if you want to go to my place and check it out and take a shower or whatever, feel free," he said.

She reached over and gave him a light cuff to the shoulder. The action was juvenile, and she recognized that, but she couldn't help herself. She didn't know how else to respond.

"Thanks for the warm invitation, but if anybody is staying anywhere between the two of us, you're going my way, not the other way around. If you only have one towel, I hate to think about your sheets situation."

He wiggled his eyebrows and his smile widened. "Yeah, you keep thinking about my sheets."

He was cute. Yet, she wasn't going to fall for any of that kind of nonsense.

She wanted to point out that he had been

clear in his plans for a relationship. And she wasn't about to start anything sexual with a man who didn't want a relationship. But what was the harm in a little no-commitment flirting?

"Do you like that?" she asked, sounding coy.

She could see him tense, and his hands moved to his knees like he was trying to ground himself. She loved that she could have that effect on him. There was nothing like leaving a man speechless.

"I wonder if they are made of cotton, satin, or hmm…maybe flannel. I can see you being a flannel sheet kind of guy," she teased.

He let out a slight chuckle. "This time of year, it's flannel all the way. In fact, if I could have them on all year, I would."

"I don't find it hard to believe."

The car in front of her moved a few inches. It wasn't even worth taking her foot off the brake. At least they had stopped to eat something before they got stuck in traffic. He took out his phone and clicked on some buttons, making her wonder if he was just as annoyed with the traffic jam as she was.

"Is this normally how you go about your surveillance?"

He looked over at her and shook his head. "Nothing about the situation has been what I would consider normal. Yet, like Muhammad Ali said, 'we all have a plan, until we get hit in the face.' Seems like no matter what the objective, and the best laid plans by my team, everything goes as it needs to. Rather than the way I would like."

"So this is abnormally normal?" She tried to make herself feel better about what an uproar she had caused in his life.

"Hardly." He paused. "Normally, I'm not the guy they send in to do this kind of surveillance. I'm more of a security guy. The trigger puller, ya know?"

That surprised her, but at the same time it didn't. He didn't seem comfortable in the role that he was playing right now, but she was glad they could be in this together. "Don't take this the wrong way, but if you're not the surveillance guy, then why didn't you ask your team to send in someone else to help?"

He looked at her like he was studying her. "Is that what you want? Someone else besides me working with you?"

His offer gave her pause. She hadn't expected his answer. What would she do without him? Without them working together to chase down their leads? They could go back to her house and she could show him her *towel* collection, but that would be far more uncomfortable than being in the crosshairs of a murderer's sights.

"Would you be more comfortable away from me?" she asked, silently praying he wouldn't say anything to hurt her.

"Never. Once I take a job, I finish it." He lifted his phone to his ear and motioned that he was making a call. "Hello, Elle?"

She could hear a woman's voice on the other end of the line.

He nodded a couple of times. "Yeah, we're stuck in traffic. I'm going to send you an address. Can you guys look into it for me and see if anyone is currently in the house? Either way, can you please set up a UAV on the target to keep an eye on her?"

Did he and his team really have the kind of resources that with a single phone call drones could be released and put on targets? The thought equally terrified and thrilled her. She had power, but she certainly didn't have weapons on speed dial.

"Yeah," he said. "I'll text you everything you need. No biggie. Great. Thanks." He hung up and glanced over at her. "They will let us know about Ms. Sanders." He texted something.

"Who is Elle?" She hadn't meant to sound jealous. She was merely wondering what role the woman he'd spoken to played in his life, but her tone was all wrong.

Based on the look on his face, he had heard her unintentional slip, as well. "Elle is my sister. My team is a small one from within the larger STEALTH group. We are part of their Shadow Team."

"Your sister?"

"Yes, my entire team is made up of my siblings. There are six of us. Like I said, small team."

"I bet it's great working with your family." She wasn't sure of what else to say.

"Some days are better than others, but all in all I can't complain. I'm a lucky man. I have a job and a team I love. I'm like a big kid most of the time."

"Did you watch a lot of *Rambo* when you were a kid or something? Was that how you got into this?"

"Ha. Yeah, something like that," he said. "Actually, it was the family business. My parents worked in this field, so it was a natural progression. After they died, it was a way for all of us to continue their legacy."

"How did they die?"

"Car accident. Well, we thought it was a car accident, but it looks like we have had people gunning for our family for a while now—Rockwood. We have reason to believe they were somehow involved with my parents' accident. But it's hard to prove. It happened a few years ago. But dollars to donuts, they killed my parents."

"I'm so sorry." She held her breath, like breathing would fill his tragedy with air again if she did.

He merely shrugged. His face hardened, like he hated talking about it as much as she hated what had happened to him and his family, but she was also grateful that he was finally beginning to really open up to her.

"Is that the company whose name was on the bombs' plates?"

"One and the same. They are corrupt and stop at nothing so long as the ends justify the means." He sighed. "Did you hear about the shooting downtown last year? The one with the sniper?"

She nodded. "That was a rough day for me. The courthouse was placed under complete lockdown and I was forced to go into the basement and seek shelter with all the other judges and officials. I had to sit with the district attorney for two solid hours. It was...*fun*."

"I can only imagine." He snorted. "Did you learn anything worthwhile from her?"

She huffed. "I had only just started as a

judge. But she said a few things that raised my hackles."

"Anything about Rockwood?" he asked, the question making her wonder what she didn't know about them.

"No. I hadn't even heard mention of them until you."

How did the company have so many enemies? What if she and Judge Hanes hadn't been the real targets? He had to have had those thoughts already, but he hadn't admitted them to her. Was that why he had stuck around? Was he worried that perhaps Rockwood was coming for him and she had just stepped into the crossfire?

No. She reminded herself that they hadn't known the company was even tangentially involved until after the bombs had gone off and they had gotten the results back. Besides, if this company was going after the Spade family, there were a million other ways they could go about it without pulling in judges and teams from the FBI.

If this company was as bad and as ruthless as Evan had alluded to, there was no way they would have done anything that would have drawn scrutiny and investigations from federal organizations. At least not on purpose.

"What did the DA say that bothered you?" he asked, forcing her from her thoughts.

"She seemed to have some kind of sense that because we were both women in a predominantly male field, that we would have some kind of quid-pro-quo deal. I had to set her straight."

"Had you met her before?" he asked.

"Not at that point, but she had a case coming up on my docket." She cleared her throat. "I don't think that she is corrupt or crooked, but I think she thought she could find more favorable treatment."

"Are you absolutely sure that was what was going on? What exactly did she say?"

She shrugged. "I don't remember what she said verbatim, but it was something to the effect of she 'hoped we could come to an arrangement' on one of her upcoming trials."

"Don't you think it is a little odd that she would say something like that?" He opened up his phone and she could see that he was looking up information about the DA.

Finally, traffic started moving again. As it did, his phone rang. "What's up?" he answered, seeming to know the caller. After a few yups and uh-huhs, he hung up.

"All okay?"

"Elle said they have signs that there is someone inside the house with the address we sent them. From the heat signature, they don't know who it is, but they think we could safely head over there."

"That is one hell of a team to have right on hand. I can't even imagine all of the capabilities you guys must have in tech and surveillance when it comes to getting things done." She paused. "I just hope you are judicious with your applications."

He chuckled. "Oh, don't worry, Judge De-Salvo. We run a little close to the line between legal and illegal, but we are always ethical."

"Unlike Rockwood?" she countered as she drove down the streets leading to Ms. Sanders's apartment.

"Exactly. I promise we are the good guys."

She believed him, but she couldn't help herself. "You know, on the bench, the bad guys are always trying to convince me that they are good guys, too."

"I'm sure that by now, even with only a year under your belt, you have learned to read people almost as well as I can."

"You do know who a murderer looks like, don't you?" she asked, a wicked half grin on her lips.

"Yeah, they look like everyone else." He snorted in what she thought was disapproval.

"Are you saying that you think I'm not on your side?"

Did she think he wasn't? Did being on her side make him a good guy?

"No," she said. "I didn't mean for the conversation to go here. I know you are doing what you think in your heart is right. I appreciate you putting your neck out for me. Truly. But I have to admit that I'm a little surprised that this Rockwood company would be sniffing around me when it seems to be very focused on you."

"I'm not sure what has happened to you has anything to do with them. If anything, I'm thinking that whoever planted those bombs… maybe they knew the Shadow Team and STEALTH would be called in. Maybe it was a message to us."

"Do you think my attacker is threatening you in order to make you stand down?"

"That's exactly what I'm beginning to think now that you and I are talking about all of this." He nodded and looked down at his phone, staring at a picture of the district attorney. She wasn't bad-looking. "When we approach Sanders's place, don't park too close. We don't want to give ourselves away."

He resumed tapping away on his phone until she pulled to a stop a block ahead of their next suspect's house.

She could see how he was drawn to this kind of work; it was thrilling to be this close to danger all the time. Though she couldn't say she loved being the one who was coming under attack. However, if she was like him and given the option to protect a civilian, she would have jumped at the chance, as well. There was power and a sense of glory in what they were doing... tracking down bad guys before they could hurt anyone again.

"This okay?" she asked.

He looked up and he appeared a bit surprised at the fact they were already there. "Yeah, this will do. I'll take point on this."

"Like last time," she said with a nod.

"May it go so smoothly."

Though she had never thought of herself as superstitious, the moment the words fell from his lips it was like she could sense a curse falling over them, shrouding them in danger.

Maybe she was just imagining things, but there was no doubt in her mind that things were about to go fifty shades of full-blown wrong.

Chapter Twelve

The door swung open before they even hit the threshold. Evan reached for his sidearm, careful to keep his draw out of view as Sophia Sanders stepped out and sneered at them. "What in the hell are you doing here?"

Natalie stopped walking and he carefully stepped around her, shielding her with his body.

"I heard you were asking around about me." Sanders was red-faced and the color seemed more vivid against the backdrop of her jet-black hair. "I don't know why you think you need to show up on my effing doorstep like I'm some kind of criminal."

"Ma'am, I don't know who you believe we are, but I can assure you that we have no intention of causing you harm." If anything, it was more that he wanted to make sure that she wouldn't hurt the woman he had come to care about. "We would just like to speak to you a little bit, ask a few questions."

"You take your lies somewhere else. I have no interest in talking. You need to leave my property, now." She pointed in the direction of their truck, like she had been sitting there watching them the whole time. It was almost as if she knew they were coming.

As he watched the woman, he noticed she barely glanced in Natalie's direction. Either she didn't want to give her bad intentions away, or she really didn't know who Natalie was. He hoped for the latter. Yet, this was their primary suspect and if she was as smart as he thought she was, she would go out of her way to keep her secrets and her crimes from being brought out into the light. For this woman, her daughter and her future were on the line. She had all the motivation in the world to act innocent.

"Did you hear me?" the woman asked. "You're not welcome here. I don't care who you are or what you think you're doing. I have nothing further to say to you, unless you show up here with a warrant or a set of handcuffs."

Maybe she wasn't so good at acting after all. She was guilty of something.

There was the rev of an engine as a Dodge Charger careened around the corner of the road and then came to a skidding, tire-screeching halt in front of the house. Ms. Rencher, Mary, stepped out and hurried toward the house.

"Damn it, Sophia, I told you not to make a scene."

Sophia let out a choking laugh and pushed past him, knocking against his elbow as he let his hand fall from his gun. Something about this didn't feel like his life was in danger, but somebody's ass was definitely going to get chewed.

"You have no business being here. I told you that you weren't to set a foot on this property ever again. You made your choices, Mary." Sophia's hands were balled into tight fists as she glared at her ex.

"Whoa," Natalie said, trying to get the women's attention. "Let's not let things get out of hand here. We were just hoping to come and—"

"Ask a few questions," Sophia said, finishing her sentence for her. "Mary told me all about you showing up at our headquarters."

"It's not *our* headquarters anymore, Sophia," Mary countered. "And, to be clear, the only reason I called you was to ask you about the order. If you have been using my accounts without my permission, you know I could have my lawyers on your ass so quick that it could make your head spin."

Evan was at a bit of a loss as to how to handle the fighting women. He wasn't sure if he should put up ropes and just let them go full

MMA or intercede in what was clearly a long-standing fight.

"If you wanted to bring in the lawyers, you know you already would have. Which means you're being cheap, you are afraid of what I am going to tell these people, or you wanted to see me." Sophia sneered. "Which is it?"

Mary strode up to Sophia, stepping so close that their noses almost touched. "We both know that if we never saw one another again, it would still be too soon."

Evan moved toward the women. "You guys are welcome to continue this fight when we leave, but I need to ask you both a few more questions."

"What?" Sophia jerked her head in his direction. "I can't believe you brought law enforcement to my house. Again. I would think you would want to protect our daughter, but it's like you thrive on this kind of drama. When are you going to grow up?"

Natalie moved by his side and gave him a look. They needed to separate the women if they were going to get any of their questions answered. He gave her a nod and moved his chin in Sophia's direction.

Natalie touched Mary's arm, and as she did Mary jerked. "What?" Anger soaked through her voice.

"I think it's best if you and Ms. Sanders took a few steps back." She gently but firmly pushed the woman back.

"Now," Evan started, "all we really need to know is who ordered those chemicals."

The women pointed at one another. Finally, Sophia spoke. "This woman wants to get me into all kinds of trouble. And the last thing I want is to have anything to do with her. I wouldn't order chemicals. Even if I had access to these accounts, I wouldn't do anything. It wouldn't even surprise me if she had done this herself and pinned it on me in hopes that I would get into trouble. I don't know if you've heard, but we are in quite a contentious divorce."

"If I had done it, why would I call you and warn you that these people were going to show up and ask you questions about it?" Mary countered. "If anything, I wanted you to be prepared. I didn't want you to get into trouble. Little Bean needs both of us. We don't have to be married anymore, but you're still her mother. We signed up for this together. Now we are in this together, forever."

Was that what this all was—some weird interfamilial drama playing out in front of them?

Sophia took a deep breath. She closed her eyes and ran her hands over her face like she was trying to dispel some of her rage. "Look, I'm sorry." She glanced at him and then at Natalie. "I didn't mean to jump down your throats when you showed up here. I just… Anytime I have to deal with her—" she pointed at her ex "—it sets my teeth on edge."

Evan nodded. "I understand how infuriating an ex can be. Relationships, especially those involving children and divorces, can be quite acrimonious."

Sophia's eyebrows rose like she was somehow impressed with his word of the day. Or maybe it was his empathy; he wasn't sure. "Obviously, things between her and me haven't been going well."

"Obviously." Mary crossed her arms over her chest and gave Sophia a sour look, one full of pain.

"There is a lot of bad blood between the two of you," Natalie said. "In my line of work, I see this kind of thing all the time, but I hope you both know that you need to be civil, especially when it comes to your child."

Sophia looked over at Natalie, finally seeming to actually notice her. "You're a cop, too?"

Is that who these women thought they were, police officers? Or was this woman just putting them on? Ignorance, in this situation, could be a great defensive move.

Though she did look unsure of them and Natalie. If he had walked into this cold and unprepared in any way, he would have believed the woman. She didn't have any indicators that she was lying, only that she was defensive—likely due to the fact her ex was standing in her front yard and they were asking her questions. But she wasn't shuffling her feet, cocking her head, or itching—all simple body language cues people exhibited when they were lying.

"Do you mind showing me the order for the chemicals you guys have been talking about?" Sophia asked, motioning toward him.

"Of course," he said, realizing that they hadn't actually given her any information about their being there.

He was glad he hadn't wasted time trying to figure out a plan when it had come to talking to this woman. Once again, they were getting punched in the face, but he had learned to take the hits and keep on fighting.

He took out his phone and opened the information. Holding up his phone, he moved closer so she could take a look at what had brought them to her doorstep in the first place.

She stared at the image for a long time. "Do you mind?" she asked, motioning to scroll the page.

"What do you need?" he asked.

"What company did we place the order with?" she asked.

He scrolled up. "It looks like it is a place called GenChem. You know them?"

A smile broke through the woman's tight features. "Ha. I know what this is." She did a small hop from one foot to the other, like an excited kid. "The company has a long-standing order with them. One on a yearly order cycle."

That made sense, but he still didn't understand why, if they didn't have a rodent problem, they were continuously using such a chemical.

"Our maintenance teams use it mostly in the alleyway and around the doors to the business. I don't know if you realize this, but there is a complete underground city beneath the streets. There, it's like the New York City sewage system with rats and vermin. If you don't stay on top of the problem, it can get bad quickly. Well, according to our company's teams..." Sophia's face soured. "I mean *your* company..." She shot Mary a hurt look.

Mary gave a stiff, acknowledging nod.

There was a long, painful pause. He had always hated this kind of breakup thing when it had been happening in his life, but it was almost as agonizing when it played out in front of him. He wished he could just talk to them both, free of emotions and pain, and see what had really come between them and see if it was fixable. But this wasn't his place. These were his suspects.

He couldn't be this tenderhearted.

For all he knew, they were in on it together and were playing him and Natalie like fools.

"I'm glad that we have all that sorted out," he said, turning off the screen on his phone. "However, given the nature of your relationship, Mary, may I ask why you warned Sophia of our coming here? And why you weren't forthcoming with the information about her current whereabouts?"

Mary looked down at the toes of her work boots.

"You know," Natalie said, jumping in, "when people hide things, it makes a person look exceedingly guilty."

He clicked his phone on and scrolled through his emails. "Mary, that is also to say nothing about the fact that you didn't send me the videos you promised me—the ones which proved you were home alone last night."

Mary's chin moved impossibly closer to her chest until there was a tiny roll of skin pinched there, under her chin.

"Are you really that embarrassed of what happened?" Sophia asked. "Just tell them. It doesn't matter. They seem like they will understand. Besides, what happened isn't worth getting in trouble over."

Mary finally looked up. "Have either of you ever gone through a messed-up, confusing-as-hell divorce?"

"Sure have, why?" he asked.

Natalie looked at him with a bit of surprise. No doubt she would have questions for him later.

"Loneliness can lead to questionable decisions." Mary held her hands together in front of her. "Not that I don't like how things went last night, Sophia…" She looked up and the two women's eyes locked.

For the first time since they had arrived, there was a degree of softness and congenial familiarity between them.

"I would hope not," Sophia said, the sound somewhat breathless.

He knew that tone. They were lost in their dance with each other. It sounded stupid, his likening their relationship to such a thing, but that was exactly what relationships were—a dance. They could be fun, inspiring, heart-warming and filled with love and laughter… and yet, if one in the pair lost their footing or got behind, it could all come to a screeching halt or a stumbling mess of disasters. They were definitely navigating the disasters, and it was all made harder by the love that still resided between the couple.

"So you guys were together last night?" Natalie asked, but he could see the twitch of a smile at the corner of her lips. Had she been rooting for the offbeat couple just like he was?

Maybe they were equally as tenderhearted as the other. That could definitely make the feelings he was having toward Natalie that much harder to dance—and he wanted the ballet.

"If you guys knew what all we have been through, you would understand why I didn't want to admit that we were together," Mary said, "but we were. And sometimes, no matter how badly someone hurts you or how badly you have hurt them, there is still just a pure, aching love between you." She smiled at Sophia. "And I don't know if we will make it or not, but I want you to know that I love you. I will always love you."

Sophia stepped over to Mary and took her hand. "I love you, too. And I'm so, so sorry. I don't think we can ever go back to what we were. There is too much water under the bridge, but maybe we could take things slow and be a team again at least for Little Bean. She needs us to be a cohesive unit."

Mary leaned into her, putting her head on Sophia's shoulder. "You got it."

From the look in the two women's eyes, this wasn't some farce.

This messy and confusing moment was real. This was love and life all wrapped into one duct-taped, wired together, big ball of the best everyone could do. It may not have been pretty, but then again maybe it was this ethereal, emotive chaos that made everything worth it.

These imperfect moments, with all their jagged edges—were what made living beautiful.

Chapter Thirteen

"That was…*raw*," Natalie said as they got back into the truck and she started driving, though she didn't even know where she should go.

"Very real," he said, looking out the window. Was he afraid that if he looked at her, what was happening between them would become real, too? "There are a lot of bombs going off there, but I don't think they were involved in any in your life."

She shook her head. "No. They aren't the kind to go after me. They are too focused on what is going on in their lives to branch out and start striking at those around them."

"Yeah, but it also means that you are still in danger. And, we're back to square one."

Her stomach sank. He was right. They could keep grasping at straws, and fighting to find who wished her harm, but the thought exhausted her. They were chasing their tails. "All

I want to do is go home and get into my bed and not move for a while."

"I get it," he said, glancing over at her. "I'm exhausted by this, too. Running on high emotions all the time can be so draining. If you need rest, let's go get some rest. We are no good if we're not thinking straight."

"I'm so glad you said that. I have really been missing my pillow." Natalie ran her hand over the back of her neck.

"Yeah, about that…" he started. "There's no way you can go back to your place. We could go to my apartment, but my family's there, and trust me, you don't want that kind of baloney. But I've got a line on a private house, if you'd like. And I know for a fact that it has great towels—a whole selection of them." He laughed.

Her entire body tightened. She had known on a certain level that the night would come again and they would be staying together, but she hadn't expected to feel this pull toward him. Could she be that close to him and keep her distance—for both of their sakes?

She had just witnessed how wrong things could go, complete with lawyers and children… houses and businesses. Did she really want to get into a relationship? A friendship with this man was far safer and smarter in the long run.

Men and women could be friends, right?

She sighed at the thought.

"No? You don't want to be alone with me?" he asked, looking over at her.

"No, that's not it," she said, waving him off. "A house would be great. Definitely smarter. I guess I can always go buy a good pillow if push comes to shove."

"We could go to a hotel, too, but I have a feeling that you would definitely need to buy a pillow in that case," he said, winking at her.

What did he mean by that? Was he thinking about them naked?

Her thoughts went to him behind her, her face pressed into a down pillow.

Stop.

Those kinds of thoughts weren't going to help her keep her hands off him.

Oddly enough, she wasn't feeling quite as tired as she had been before.

"Yeah, a house is good. Separate bedrooms." She sounded clipped.

"Yes," he said.

His quick agreement bit at her. He hadn't even had to think about it. Did he not want her, at all? She should have never let him kiss her. When would she learn? As soon as a man got a taste, it was like they no longer had any need to pursue. And if they'd had sex he probably would have left her in the middle of the night—

regardless of his proclamations and promises to keep her safe.

Men.

He clicked away on his phone, making her miss hers all that much more. How nice it would be to pick it up and escape for a while. Though that was what she had loved best about giving it up in the first place.

She thought about all the work waiting for her as soon as she came back online—no doubt she would have to answer more questions about Judge Hanes and she'd probably have to take over some of his cases if he didn't get back on his feet soon. Being here, with Evan, was simpler in all the ways that didn't involve her heart.

"I just got word that your friend, the judge, has woken up."

She smiled. "Thank goodness. I'm so glad. How is he doing?"

"They said he is not making a whole lot of sense yet, but he is gaining ground each passing hour." He paused. "But they are worried about him being a fall risk. Apparently, he keeps talking about getting up and walking out. He is pretty out of it."

"I'm just glad he's alive. Do you think he will make a full recovery?"

"Nerve agents can have some long-lasting effects. And none of them are good. If he ends up being able to even go back home within the next few months that would be a real positive."

She knew he was right, and yet she hated it. "Are you sure there isn't any way we can find out about the sarin?"

"I talked to Agent Hart. He's looking into that from his side. But I haven't heard anything on that line yet." Evan shrugged.

She hated how little progress they had made and if they went to go see the judge, she wanted to give him some kind of good news—that they were no longer going to have to worry about their personal safety. Instead, the next time she saw him, she would only be the bearer of bad news.

It was terrible, but she was somewhat glad Steve Hanes wouldn't be able to understand. She could at least save him some of the anguish of knowing that whoever attacked him was still on the loose.

The only comfort she could find in any of this was that if the attackers still wanted Judge Hanes to be dead, at least he was being watched over by the other Spade family members. If Evan's siblings were anything like him, there was no way Hanes was going to be left alone. They couldn't always stop the bad things from happening—that was outside anyone's ability as long as the perpetrator was on the loose—

but at least they would do everything in their power to keep Steve safe, and to get information from him when he was capable of speaking coherently.

Until she saw him, though, at least she could rest.

The house where Evan took her was high up on a mountain, overlooking the city nestled into the valley floor. She hadn't grown up in the city; rather, her familial home had been about fifty miles down in the Bitterroot Valley near Hamilton, Montana. Both were tucked into the mountains where they were protected from the extreme cold and heat that much of the eastern side of the state would encounter. She'd always loved those mountains. They were the backbone of the United States, and if she was to pick the heart it would have been the city whose lights were reflecting off the clouds above them.

As they pulled up to the house, she was surprised. She had expected a rental that was like some little dingy pillbox house near the university campus, where they would bump against each other while passing in the hall. And yet, the house that stood before her was a grand log home. Inside, someone had left the light on, and through the living room window, she could see an antler chandelier and a buffalo blanket adorning the far wall. It looked far more like a hunting lodge than a city dwelling.

Whoever their interior designer was, she needed to hire them. This place was the epitome of Montana living. Many out-of-staters yearned to move here after seeing homes just like this one. There was just something about being perched on the top of the mountain overlooking the quaint city on one side and the wild on the other. It was like a metaphor for life.

Evan got out and opened her door for her. She pulled her jacket tight, blocking the wind as they walked up the stone walkway into the house. Snow had drifted into the corners of the entryway and she found it a bit soothing—nature was gently battling with mankind's intrusions. She loved this home, but nature's subtle war reminded her of her own. Over time, eventually she would go back to nature just like this place. In the meantime, she could let the weaker souls wear away while she stood strong. She only had so many days left on this planet, and she'd make the most of every single one of them.

"I hope you like the place. We even have a bottle of wine ready, if you're interested." He pressed a series of numbers on the door lock, and it clicked open.

She'd be more than happy to have a glass of wine and just relax. It wasn't maybe the smartest thing to do given the circumstances, but she didn't care. Sometimes enjoying life meant knowing when to relax. They had been going nonstop all day and had started the morning off with yet another threat. She needed a little time. Maybe it would help her to make sense of things, and maybe she could unpack some of the feeling she had been trying to stuff away. At times like these, it was impossible to deal with everything right in the moment.

"Do you think there's a chance of the perpetrator finding us again?" she asked.

He shrugged. "I know you said you thought no one would find you at your mom's place, but if someone had really done their research into you, I think it would've been easy enough for them to track us down. So for tonight I think you can relax."

"Didn't you say that when you're at your most comfortable, that is also when you are in the most danger?" she asked, a playful grin on her face.

"How dare you use my words against me?" he teased. "But yes, you're right and I didn't say that I would be relaxed. I just think you could."

He opened the door, and the hinges didn't even make a sound. As they walked inside, the place smelled like cinnamon sticks and apples.

Though they had eaten not that long ago, it made her mouth water.

Her first impression of the log home paled in comparison to the charming entryway. It had at least a twenty-foot cathedral ceiling, complete with slate floors, which led into a variety of rooms. In the living room, there was a crackling fire in the river-rock fireplace. It was an open floor plan; the only thing dividing the living room from the kitchen was a large quartz countertop. Even from this far away, she could make out glittering flecks of gold in its surface. The cabinetry in the kitchen was built of natural wood, with curls and knots in their surfaces. Though they were a shade lighter than the surrounding log walls, they were perfectly offset.

The place was breathtaking.

At the center of the counter in the kitchen was a large bouquet of red roses and white lilies. The arrangement had always been her favorite and it made her wonder if someone had known, or if it was just one of those odd coincidences that happened in life.

As he closed the door behind them, she walked to the flowers and gently ran her finger along the silky edge of the lily. Was this all some kind of message, a sign? Did she even believe in signs? Some days she thought such things were complete drivel; if a person looked for something hard enough, they would always find it…good or bad. This time, though, she had a surge deep in her belly that made her wonder if she had just been forced by the universe to face the fact she had been brought to this place, this time with this man all for a reason. It felt almost as though she was meant for this. What exactly *this* was, however, was still up in the air.

He had made it clear he didn't want a relationship, and she had made some of the same arguments, but the heart wanted what the heart wanted. There were few words that could make two souls, who wanted to love one another, stop from loving. But just because her soul called to his, it didn't guarantee that his did for her.

He had seemed attracted to her, but maybe he had rebuffed a relationship with her out of some misguided kindness to cover his change of heart. If he wasn't attracted to her, it would have been so much easier for her if he just came out with it—or, maybe not. His saying "I'm not attracted to you" would hurt, too.

He walked past her and washed his hands in the sink. After drying them, he went to the stainless-steel fridge and opened the door. Inside was a bottle of chardonnay and a plate with a bow atop. Taking them out, he then placed the bottle and the plate next to the flowers.

Unwrapping the cellophane revealed a circle of soft cheese, smoked salmon and an array of crackers.

"Whoever your friends are that own this place, I am going to need to meet them." She took a cracker and added a bit of cheese and fish to the top and popped it into her mouth.

"The owner is pretty cool," he said. "And keeps the place well stocked."

She could tell he was holding back something, but she didn't mind that he wanted to keep his relationship with them quiet. Her life was forced to be treated in much the same way. Thanks to her variety of roles in the legal system over the years, she had learned more secrets about people than she had ever thought possible, secrets she would never share.

Yet, that didn't stop her from being slightly curious if the person who owned this home was another contractor like Evan, or if they were a client. If she had to guess, she would say client. No contractor would live this…this *boldly*.

"Is your apartment anything like this?" she asked as he opened a drawer and pulled out a corkscrew.

"Ha. No." He shook his head. "There, I live with my family and my team. But it is nice to have a private place to crash when I need a break, so I keep an apartment on the side."

His *family*; the word echoed in the high-peaked room.

"Have you ever thought about having a family? You know, kids with your ex or anything?" she said, bringing up the subject with tiptoeing words.

"We talked about it, but we had gotten married so young and we both agreed that we didn't want kids. We just wanted a life full of adventures and travel." He paused. "In the end, she changed her mind. Adventure begins to lose its allure after a while. Even travel does. At a certain point, what you yearn for the most is to be home with the people you love."

"But if you don't mind me saying, wasn't she the person you loved—your family?" She cocked her head to the side and ended up hoping he would hear the question for what it was and not perceive it as some kind of needling.

He rolled his lips together like he was trying to keep from saying something, or possibly he was just thinking. "I believe that ideally your spouse should be. And I think that for most people that would be true. But she and I… We should have never gotten married. We're still friends, though. But even as friends, going through divorce is tough. I'm not one who likes to fail."

"Just because you got divorced, it doesn't

mean you failed." She scowled at such a ridiculous idea. "There are a million reasons cou-
ples don't make it. I've heard most of them.
Choosing to walk away from one another is far
harder than staying in a relationship you know
isn't working. In fact, I think that you call your
divorce a success. You're still friends. That's
admirable. It means that you chose, as two respectful adults, to accept that your relationship
wasn't a good fit. It's astounding to me the number of people who try to force a marriage to
work and then end up hating each other."

He nodded but she could see that he still
struggled with feeling like a failure.

"Besides," she continued, "if you had stayed,
can you imagine how different your life would
be?"

He stuffed a bite of cracker into his mouth.
He popped open the wine bottle, grabbed two
glasses from the cupboard and poured them
each a healthy glass. He handed hers over.
"What about you? Any successes or failures?
You know, in relationships or whatever?"

"I…" She didn't know how much she wanted
to tell him. If she opened up to him and let him
know exactly how mundane her life had been,
would he lose interest—this man of adventure?
"I haven't had a lot of serious relationships.
Never been married. I have been asked, but I

have always been so focused on my work and my goals that I failed in my relationships."

He huffed out a laugh. "I can respect that."

She smooshed her lips, dispelling some of the tension from the air. "Yeah, I'm a crappy girlfriend and I knew I'd make a crappy wife."

"Why would you say that?" He looked at her with genuine interest, like he couldn't possibly understand why she would have said something like that about herself.

She shrugged, even though she knew the innumerable reasons and arguments that she could put forth in order to validate her assessment. "Like I said, I've never been very good at putting my partner first."

"That's crazy."

She scowled. "What is crazy about it? It's in every relationship how-to book and every episode of midday television…you have to put your loved ones first in order for your love for one another to survive."

He seemed to once again scoff at the idea. "Don't get me wrong…" he started. "I love Dr. Phil-isms as much as the next person, but who says we have to conform our love and our lives to what society deems as 'perfect' or 'ideal'? You and I are cut from a different cloth. What if we were going to be together? I would never expect you to put me before your job. Ever."

She didn't know what to say.

"Seriously. What you are doing with your life…you are making a difference in the world. Who would dare to ask you to stop putting yourself and your work first in order to affirm your love for them? You love them or you don't. You don't seem like the kind of woman who would mince words or waste time."

She couldn't possibly have been hearing him right. Men, especially alpha types, were rarely this progressive when it came to relationships. In fact, the few men she had dated—mostly cops—had been more of the caveman type. She was lucky not to have been clubbed when they had tried to take her back to their caves for the night. What had made those dates even more frustrating was the fact that they knew exactly who she was, what she wanted in her future and where her priorities lay and yet, it was like they didn't know those things when they were finally over their initial phases of lust. Then both men had wanted her to settle down, to conform.

They were left wanting.

"Are you screwing with me right now? Telling me what you think I want to hear?" she said, taking a sip of the wine.

"No. Because I feel the same way. I mean what I say. I can change my mind about many things, but once I tell someone I love them, I love them forever."

She wasn't sure how she felt about the thought of him still loving his ex-wife—most women would have been jealous, and maybe she was a touch, but mostly she found it endearingly sweet. Throughout a person's life, they loved many people—lovers, family and even friends. To think that he would give it forever, no matter what happened between them, that was incredible. She cherished the thought that a person whose love was so pure and unending was in her life. Not that he loved her. But to think he was capable...

She needed more wine.

She took a long drink, emptying her generously filled glass. He poured her another as soon as she sat the glass back down. She was glad she didn't have to go through the questions of "do you want another" and then feel like she had to pretend to be in favor of temperance. It was like he knew what she wanted without her speaking. She could get used to this.

"About work before love," he said, taking a drink from his glass and setting the bottle down. "We need to go over the other people who've ordered the chemical. And I should check in with the FBI. They might have more info by now."

She nodded, and then had to stifle a yawn. Despite her pleasure at being in this home with him, the day was taking its toll.

He must have noticed.

"We're tired, and won't be at our best. It can wait till the morning."

"Okay," she said. "But go on—about work and love and priorities."

"I didn't want to give the impression I think either of us should not value the other more than their job. I'm just saying that it's okay for your priorities to be on succeeding in life. Happiness in one area of your life tends to lead to happiness in all the others."

Did he say us?

She smiled at him, her chest threatening to explode with joy. "I never realized what a philosopher you were. I like it."

Though it was probably the endorphins or dopamine hitting her brain and making her feel a rush, as his gaze settled on her and his lips pulled into that sexy smile, she didn't care what the physiological reason was for her yearning to touch him. All she wanted to do was reach out, pull him between her thighs and kiss his lips until they were both unable to do anything but bask in the flavor of the other.

"I'm no philosopher, but I definitely have seen enough of life to know my way around it.

Though I'm more than aware others may have different perspectives than myself." He looked down at his wineglass.

Was he worried that she felt differently than he did? How could she? Everything he had said so far made complete sense to her. If anything, it was almost as if he could read her mind. Or was telling her what she wanted to hear, like she assumed before.

"I think an indicator of a good relationship is one that brings out the best in both people."

He nodded but had a contemplative look on his face. "I agree, but I think it's impossible for two people to expect perfection from each other. While you can bring out the best in each other, in a relationship I think you can also expect to bring out the worst. It's how you deal with those moments of weakness that separates you from who makes it and who doesn't."

"What do you think is your greatest weakness?" she asked.

As soon as she asked the question, she wondered if that was the most prudent thing she could have done. Oftentimes, the best thing a person could do was remain silent. But if they were really going to seek a relationship with one another, like she hoped they would, she needed to know the weaknesses in his case along with the strengths.

He took another long drink of his wine and then refilled his glass. "Do you want an indexed list, or would you prefer the top ten?" He chuckled.

"Hit me with your best shot," she teased, quoting one of her favorite '80s songs.

"Okay, Pat Benatar." He laughed, throwing his head back.

As he moved, she caught sight of a few silvery hairs in the dark underbelly of his beard. Damn. He was so damned sexy.

"I guess if I had to pick my worst fault... I would say that I can be super hard on myself. I mean, look at this situation. I feel *terrible* that I haven't been able to keep you completely out of harm's way. When we get through this, and I know we will, I am going to go over every turn of events at least a thousand times in my head. I will pick it apart and overthink—all so I don't make the same mistakes."

"Like kissing me?" she asked, looking down at the flecks of gold in the countertop and running her finger along the stem of her wineglass.

"That is one thing I will definitely be replaying in my mind for the rest of time, but not because it was a mistake. Rather, I will wonder how I got to be so lucky."

Heat rose in her face and she was embarrassed by such an adolescent response as her blush deepened. What a vicious cycle.

"If anyone is lucky here, it is me in meeting you. You may not see it this way, but if you hadn't walked into Hanes's office when you did, it's very likely that I would have died—possibly either way—by now. You saved my life."

He looked away, humbled. "That's not true. If I would have shown up a few minutes earlier, maybe neither of you would have fallen into harm's way."

"It's unfortunate about the judge, but even if you had been there earlier...he still would have fallen under attack." Emboldened by the wine or maybe his words, she reached over and put her hand on his. "You couldn't have seen that coming. It was an innocuous thing. No one would be wary of a pen. None of this is your fault."

"It happened on my watch."

"That doesn't matter. A lot of things happen independently of us. We just have to deal with the consequences. I would like to say it's indicative of our jobs, but I think everybody has exactly the same problem. Everyone in the world is just doing the best they can after what some other person has done to them."

He twisted his hand so he could take hold of her fingers. "At least there has been something good to come of all of this." Leaning forward, he kissed her knuckles, his hair brushing against her skin and making goose bumps rise on her arms.

Her mind went straight to all the other places she would love to feel his beard scrape against her.

He looked up, his mouth still on her skin, and his cheek lifted with his smile. His eyes were devilish. Even if she hadn't secretly loved him before, that look and she would have been done for. She was his.

"Do you even know where the bedrooms are in this place?" she asked, not bothering to beat around the proverbial bush.

He nodded, taking her hand and motioning for her to grab her glass of wine.

She walked behind him as he led her upstairs and to the large bedroom at the end of the hall. "Wait." She stopped, trying to fight the buzz of the wine to bring forward some amount of lucid thought.

She couldn't jump into bed with him just because she wanted to…and he wanted to. There was no real rush if they wanted to be together.

"I know we talked about this before, and I know it's going to be a major mood killer, but if we do this… I don't want it to be a one-night thing."

He smiled back at her, the same look in his

eyes as when he had kissed her downstairs. "Me neither."

"So if this happens…we…you and I are going to *do* this whole *relationship* thing?" she asked, suddenly more nervous than when she had been thinking about having sex with him.

He stopped abruptly and turned to face her. He put his arms around her waist and she followed suit. They stared into each other's eyes. "I hate that you have to look at the world like that. I mean, I understand why. I get that sex has turned into an item of convenience. But it hasn't for me. I don't just have sex with anyone. If we're going to do this it means that I care for you, and you care for me. And I want a relationship."

Though it was the last thing she wanted to do, she could feel tears forming in her eyes. Thankfully, he didn't seem to notice.

"Now, do I think the relationship is a great idea? No. But like you said, love isn't convenient. Relationships aren't always convenient. But I think that in this world, where two people who meet and actually have the same feelings toward one another is completely unusual, I would like to give it a try. What do you think?"

She wanted to jump in with both feet. She wanted to press her lips against his and shut him up right then and there. She wanted him to promise her forever. And yet, the realist in her—the one who had seen the most heinous crimes and terrible pain—kept her from doing so. The cynic in her reminded her what a bad idea all relationships were, even with the man of her dreams.

There was no such thing as a perfect person. And right now she was so enraptured by this man that she had to have been blind. He told her his greatest fault was that he was too hard on himself. So how would that affect their relationship? Would he always be the whipping boy? Would he be able to bring equal power in the relationship? What if she was more controlling than he was, or he was more controlling than she was? She couldn't be with somebody who wasn't her equal.

He moved closer, brushing his lips against the side of her cheek. "Don't overthink this. I know that face. I make that face. And when it comes to things like this, matters of the heart, sometimes you just have to go with your feeling. And right now all I want to do is make love to you."

He scooped her up into his arms and carried her to the master bedroom.

Even if she had been tempted to continue questioning what was happening, she could do so no longer.

"How do you know your way around this house so well? Do you bring a lot of women to this place?" she teased, giggling.

"This house is actually mine. It's the only secret I have. No one knows about this place. I bought it a year ago and I hide away here when I can't be around my family for another second. A lot of times they think I'm working, but really, I'm up here watching television and vegging out. I love them, but they can be a lot."

"Wait..." She put her hand on his chest. "You *own* this place? Are you messing with me? This is my *dream house*."

He answered with a huge smile. "Mine, too. And you are the one and only person I have ever had here. I haven't even let a delivery man in this place."

She wasn't sure how such a thing would be possible, but she believed him. "I'm honored."

"I just hope you like my bedroom. It's a bit of a man cave. I never intended on having a woman up here. Well, to be more accurate, I had no plans to bring anyone here, not just a woman."

Now he was the one blushing.

She sat up slightly in his arms and kissed his lips as he carried her over the threshold of his bedroom. She closed her eyes, savoring the juxtaposition between his soft lips and his coarse beard. She'd never dated anyone with facial hair before. This was something totally new. Reaching up, she ran her fingers through it. "I love this." She gripped his hair, giving it a gentle tug.

He grumbled.

Holding her with one arm, he reached up and pulled her hair, exposing her neck to his kiss. He starting kissing at the base of her ear and moved down her neck, making an electric charge move through her body. Her core clenched as the wetness grew.

How had *she* gotten so lucky?

She was in the house of her dreams with a man so hot she wasn't certain she could have even imagined him or described him to her friends. And yet, here he held her and he was kissing her neck.

All clear thoughts left the building. The only thing she could think of was the feeling of his tongue as it flicked her earlobe and mixed with the heat of his breath in her ear. She wanted to make love to him right in this second, but at the same time she ached to hold out…to make him kiss every part of her before she let him take her.

She wanted to make him earn her and to want her so badly that the moment he slipped inside he would beg for release—and she would make him wait.

Yeah, maybe she was a bit of a control freak in and out of the bedroom, but she loved every damned second of it.

He moved to the bed and set her down. She was enveloped by the thick down comforter, complete with little red reindeer. His bed looked like something out of Santa's mansion, complete with big, fur-covered and red-quilted pillows. She ate it up.

Laying her down, he moved to her pants and carefully undid the top button. "I'm afraid I don't have anything for you to wear." He passed her an impish grin. "I hope you are okay with that."

She was dripping. "I…" She struggled to find words as his hands worked her zipper down and slipped her pants free of her legs. "I…won't…"

"Hmm?" he asked, cocking his head to one side. "Having a hard time finding your words?" he teased, tiptoeing his fingers up the insides of her thighs and tracing them back down toward her knees.

He had to see the wetness soaking through her panties by now.

Had she shaved her legs?

Crap. She couldn't remember. Hopefully, he wouldn't care.

And… Whatever. This wasn't only about his satisfaction.

Her entire life, when it came to sex, all she had ever cared about was pleasing her partner. But why? It wasn't hard to make men happy. Why couldn't she seek her own satisfaction in this moment? Undoubtedly, if she found the ending she wanted, he would, too. And better, he would get to know that he had made her feel something so beautiful.

As he opened up the buttons of her shirt and kissed her naked skin, she thought about all the pain and hate in the world. They had both seen so much evil. It was moments like this, where two souls connected and shared in this special secret, that brought goodness to life.

Yes, she was going to live this moment up. If it was to be the first time of many or the last time she was to feel his lips on her skin, she was here. This was love.

Could love live in a single moment? Or was this something else? Was it only lust?

He had said he wanted a relationship, but if this was only to be tonight, she would have to tell herself it had only been lust. But right now all she felt was love.

His tongue found her center, over her panties. She gasped. He pushed them to the side and his tongue flicked against her nub. She nearly quivered with excitement. Oh, it had been so long.

He pressed his tongue inside her and then moved up, circling her with the tip of his tongue before flicking her, hard. She jumped, loving every second of it. She relaxed back into the bed, letting him explore her body. This was for him, too.

But what if he didn't like her?

What if she tasted bad?

She put her arm over her head. Why? Why did she have to have these thoughts when all she wanted to do was to let herself savor the moment? All she had to do was feel and yet, all she could do was think.

What in the hell was wrong with her?

Stop. She had to stop this crazy spiral of thoughts.

Be present.

She sighed as she ran her fingers through his blond hair. He pressed his mouth down on her.

Flick.

Roll.

Dip.

She gasped. Yes. That. She loved *that*. Whatever *that* was that he was doing to her.

He pulled her into his mouth and sucked. And just when she thought it couldn't feel better, he flicked.

If she died in this moment, she would have been satisfied with her life.

How. Yes. Oh. Yes.

"I…" she started, but she was stopped as he sucked and flicked again.

Seriously, she had no idea what he was actually doing to her body, but it felt better than anything she had ever felt in her entire life.

"You…"

"Yes?" he asked, finally releasing her.

"You. Are. The. Best," she said between ragged, wanting breaths.

"And so are you." He dove down, back between her legs.

Her legs shook as he pulled her into his mouth and pushed his fingers inside her. She lifted her hips, letting him push deeper into her.

More. She needed more.

Reaching down, she let him know what she wanted. She rolled on her side and guided him into her. He eased into her gently though she was more than ready to take every bit of what he graciously offered. She took hold of his muscular ass and pressed him into her, throwing her head back as he took control of her and made her gasp.

After a moment he rolled on top of her. He looked into her eyes as he slowed, letting her feel every sensation…the feel of him between her legs, the heat of his breath, the dampness of their skin as they pressed against one another.

He picked up his speed and she pressed her face into his neck, kissing him and nibbling as if she could taste the ecstasy as it edged close. His breathing quickened and she could feel him grow harder within her.

"Not yet," she begged.

"Yes. This. Is. For you." He stopped, collecting himself.

He moved to sitting and lifted her legs so they rested over the tops of his shoulders. He moved slow, controlled. Using the tip, he ran it over her, playing. He eased into her again.

Putting her hands on the cold wooden headboard, she pressed herself down on him. Now it was her turn to take control.

Rocking her hips, she used one hand to help herself, making him watch.

"Yes," he begged. "Please." His words sounded ragged and heavy as he waited for her. "Let's do this together, baby. Please."

A low primal sound escaped her throat as she let go.

This. Him. Now. All of this. She wanted him. All of him. And not just now; she wanted him, always. As it seemed, he was more than happy to give it all.

Chapter Fourteen

Evan could think of no moments better than those he and Natalie had shared. They had barely slept and when they weren't making love, they were lying in bed next to each other, talking and laughing. If he could have, he would have stayed in that moment forever. In those hours, nothing else but her mattered.

And damn if he didn't love her. Hard.

He'd wanted to tell her last night, but he'd stopped himself several times. In the sheets was hardly the right time to tell someone you loved them for the first time. It should be *real*, not expressed when a person was so filled with happy hormones that they could love a toaster and mean it. Natalie was far too special to just blurt it out.

Thinking of special, he hoped he had made her feel that she was special to him last night. He had pulled out all the stops in satisfying her and he had given it a solid college try to kiss every inch of her entire body. Though he had no doubts she had enjoyed herself—he would need to throw the sheets in the wash later—he hoped she knew that he had never had a night like they had shared ever before. And he doubted that he would ever have a night as good as it again. This was the best first, and hopefully the last.

He sat out a cup of coffee and a plate of biscuits and gravy for her on the kitchen island and when she finally appeared, freshly showered, she smiled and gobbled it down. She barely took a breath and he was glad that she appreciated his cooking.

"Want any more?" he asked.

She shook her head as she took a long pull from her coffee mug.

"Are you sure? I know I worked you over pretty hard last night," he teased, his thoughts moving to how good she had looked on top of him with her hair falling down over her shoulders.

His body was tired, but apparently, not too tired.

"I'm fine. I was just hoping we could hit the ground running today. Oddly enough, I'm feeling reinvigorated," she said, sending him a cute grin over the lip of her coffee mug.

"Glad to hear it. I'd hate to have to help you

find a renewal of energy again sometime. Or, I can ask Judy for one of her special breakfasts."

They laughed. "Oh, she is going to love our being together."

"Definitely. You want to go check on her soon?" He made sure to stand well covered behind the counter.

"Not until we find my attacker. I was hoping we could maybe look into the rest of the list of chemical buyers today."

"Great minds," he said, leaning slightly to adjust himself. He walked around the counter and gave her a kiss to the head. "Let's hit it."

It didn't take them long to get to the main fire station downtown and be buzzed in. The place was awash with the sounds of men talking and a blaring television. The place smelled like old smoke and a chemical he couldn't quite put his finger on, but something oily. The door from the main lobby to the garage was open and from where he stood, he could make out the sounds of a basketball bouncing and the clink and rattle as someone made a basket.

The place reminded him of a military base with men making dark but damn funny jokes. The only thing missing was the sounds of rounds being pinged off in the distance. A woman walked around the corner and gave them an acknowledging tip of the head. "Can I point you in some kind of direction?" she asked.

"Actually," he started, "we were hoping to talk to Mr. VanBuren. He working today?"

"Hmm…yeah. He is not normally here on the weekends, but I think I saw him poking around in his office earlier. I think he was filling in for our battalion chief. Follow me." She led them down a white-tiled hallway and deeper into the building until they came to a row of glass-walled offices and a large classroom at the end.

To their left, sitting in his office and leaning back in his chair while he chatted on the phone, was a man with VanBuren on the nameplate affixed to his white uniform shirt. He looked up as they stopped. He frowned, looking a bit put out that he was being bothered. The woman motioned they were there to see him. He lifted his finger, said something to the person he was talking to on the phone, then hung up and waved them in.

"Have a good one," the firefighter said as she turned and went back to the main area.

"Thanks again," Natalie said.

"No prob," the woman called behind her.

VanBuren opened his office door and poked his head out. His hair was almost completely gray, but there was a smattering of brown through it. His eyes were red, like he hadn't had a great deal of sleep. "What can I do for you?" He looked over at Natalie and stared for a moment, almost as if he was trying to place her. "Judge DeSalvo? What are you doing down here?"

She gave the man a warm smile, but her face was tight like she didn't really know him. "Actually, I don't know if you heard, but my car was bombed a couple of days back."

"Oh yeah," VanBuren said, walking out into the hall. "Bad business. Has the FBI made any progress on tracking down the individual responsible?"

She shook her head. "Not yet, but they are working on it."

"Glad to hear you were safe. You have any ideas who would have done something like that? I got word that Hanes got hurt that day, as well. Any word on his condition?" the man asked.

"He's going to survive," Evan said, looking the man in the eyes.

"Glad to hear." VanBuren looked away and Evan tried not to read too much into it.

This man was on their short list of suspects, but it didn't mean much and it was normal for people to avoid eye contact, especially when one or both were feeling at all uncomfortable. And, no doubt, standing in front of the district court judge would make anyone working under the umbrella of the city a little bit nervous. Evan wondered if VanBuren had ever had to sit in or testify in her court. Even if he hadn't, it was probably only a matter of time until he did.

"I know your station was the one that took the call for the bombing," Natalie said. "Did you hear anything about what had happened or about the bomb itself?"

The man shrugged. "Not a whole lot. Our investigator worked with the FBI in pulling together what he could, but I haven't talked to him. Why?"

Evan tried to disarm him by leaning against the wall and letting out a long yawn before speaking. "Well, one of the chemicals in the bomb was something you are on record as ordering."

"Huh. What?"

"Zinc phosphide," Natalie answered.

"Ah, yeah. I use it in my training." The man looked slightly relieved, like he was afraid they were going to ask him straight out if he had helped to make the device. "We were working on Class D fires a few weeks ago with a few of the rookies and younger guys."

Evan had once heard that most firefighters were arsonists at heart. To battle fire, a person had to love it. It was right in line with cops being one different choice away from being criminals. He believed it, but according to that logic he would have been one step away from being a murderer; that was a hard pill to swallow.

"How did the training go?" Natalie asked, seeming genuinely interested. "What did you do?"

"Just the normal thing. I created a fire in our tower. Made them establish what kind of fire it was and how best to battle it. The different teams did well, but they still need a little more work before I'll be satisfied." VanBuren shrugged. "Why?"

Natalie looked like she was going to answer, so Evan stopped her by saying, "How many did you have in your teams?"

"Well, let's see…" The man stared into space and said a few names aloud. "Oh, and there was Lewis and Barber. Oh…and Hanes."

"Hanes? Sven Hanes?" Evan asked.

The man nodded, but there was a flicker of annoyance on his face and he ran his hand over his mouth. "The one and only."

What was that supposed to mean? Did the man dislike the judge's son? He wanted to press him and ask him about his feelings directly, but he knew that the man's loyalty—regardless of his personal feelings—would always be with his fellow firefighters and not some stranger off the street.

Natalie nodded, seeming to have noticed the man's body language, as well. "I've heard mixed reviews on that kid. How is it going with him?"

The man looked directly at Evan before peering back at the judge. "Meh. Hard to say. He's only been with us about a year and I don't work with him a whole lot, other than on the training stage. We will see his stuff when he hits the big leagues."

Evan wasn't sure exactly what the man meant by that. He would have assumed that all firefighting was dangerous and *big league*, but he didn't bother to ask.

"He's smart, though?" Natalie continued. "Quick to learn?"

The man shrugged. "He's been having some personal problems that are getting in the way of his reaching his full potential, if you ask me. But when he gets his ducks in line, there will be hope for him. Maybe."

"What kind of personal problems?" he asked.

The man lifted his hand as he shrugged. "Relationship things according to the gossip I've picked up, but there is talk of more. How

much validity there is in the rumor mill, well…
you know."

He could tell, based on the indifference on
the man's face, that either he didn't know much
more about Sven or wasn't about to divulge
what he did know.

"Do you mind showing us the zinc phosphide?" Natalie asked, sounding endearingly
curious.

The guy looked at her like she was crazed,
but he shrugged. "Not much to see, really."

"I sure would appreciate it," she said, touching his shoulder like he was a lock and her fingers were the key.

It was great watching her in action. She was
smooth when it came to her getting what she
wanted without the other person realizing. Had
she used the same moves on him? He almost
shook his head. It was impossible. He had come
into her life and wanted things and he couldn't
think of her asking him for anything…well,
other than in bed last night.

He smiled at the thought. There she could
make him do anything she liked.

VanBuren led them out of the hall of offices,
talking to Natalie quietly as he followed behind. They walked through the garage where
the crew was still playing basketball and didn't
even seem to notice intruders in their midst.

The officer opened up a large door, which led to a concrete room filled with a variety of canisters and boxes stacked on a series of steel shelves that lined the walls. In the back corner of the long, thin room, was a white five-gallon bucket on the floor.

"I used most of it, but left enough for one more burn." VanBuren went over and pointed at the bucket, seeming to think that it was the bucket they wished to see.

"Do you mind opening it for me? I am just curious to see what it looks like." Natalie smiled.

He could see the man lose brain cells at the smile. He'd always known that women had a magical power to make a man lose his mind, but it had been a while since he had seen it on display.

VanBuren pulled out a pocketknife and made quick work of unlatching the thick plastic lid. "Huh."

"What is it?" Natalie asked.

"I would say about half of what I left is missing." The man looked at them like they knew something he didn't, and he didn't appreciate it. "How did you guys know I was going to find it like this?"

"To be honest, we were grasping at straws here. Just running down a list, you know. In fact, we thought we'd find nothing with you or the department." Evan sighed.

"About Hanes…" The man looked down at the bucket. He shook the contents as if doing so would magically make more appear. "If you think he's got something to do with what's been going on around town here, I can't say…but what I can say is that he works with lots of chemicals. He and I have done a heck of a lot of training exercises and…well, if he has gone off the rails, he could be a real dangerous man."

Chapter Fifteen

They sat on the steps of the Federal building, waiting for the FBI agent who was supposed to be meeting them soon. The Bureau had been amenable to their help, thanking them for the assistance with the case, but she had a feeling the agent she had spoken to on the phone had been rolling his eyes while she had been talking.

She was happy to wait out in the cool air, if it meant she didn't have to get pulled into some flurry of politics. Evan, on the other hand, kept looking around, and she knew he was scoping out the area for trouble. He'd wanted to wait inside.

She would much rather lean against Evan, relax into him like she had last night.

Stepping out of his magnificent house this morning had been a slap back to reality. It had been so nice to escape with him. He had nearly worn her out, not that she would have ever admitted that she was anything less than a sexual dynamo who was capable of demigod stamina and insatiability—at least not to him.

The thought made her smile. Yes. Demigod, that was what she was. Albeit one who feared losing control. Though, thinking of it, wasn't that what most Greek figures had struggled with, as well?

"What are you smiling about?" he asked, nudging her knee with his.

She looked at him. "I was just nerding out for a minute."

"How nerdy did you go?" he asked.

"I was dipping into thoughts of Phobos."

He cocked a brow as he looked to her. "As in the god of fear?"

"And there I was, wondering if you were just a door kicker." She touched the side of his leg with the back of her hand. "You are always surprising me."

"Oh, honey, you ain't seen nothing yet."

The front door of the Federal building opened up and the secretary who had met them when they first arrived looked out. "Hey, guys," he said, looking apologetic. "I hate to tell you this but Agent Hart can't get away from his desk right now. I'm sorry. He requested you guys go pick up some late breakfast and he will catch up with you at his earliest convenience."

She gave a stiff nod. "Fine." She stood up and brushed the bits of snow off the back of her pants. She was angry, but she wasn't about to lose her patience on the messenger.

"Tell him lives hang in the balance," Evan said, annoyed. "We will be waiting for him."

The man nodded and disappeared behind the doors.

"So what are we going to do?" she asked.

"On a positive note, if the agent assigned to our case is this busy, then I think it's fair to say he is giving your case the attention it requires. I hope."

She wasn't a federal court judge, so she didn't usually work directly with the FBI, but she found it hard to believe they wouldn't come to her aid with the same level of professionalism and professional courtesy as if she was one. There had to have been something else going on.

"I hope you're right about that," she said, waving him off. "From what I know about those who work behind those doors, they are a good crew."

He ran his hands over his face. "I know… one of my brothers is married to one of their former agents."

She gaped at him. "What?"

"Yeah, Kate Scot is Troy's wife."

"How have you not told me your sister-in-law was an agent?"

"Actually, she still is one, but she's working out of Kirtland in New Mexico. I think she probably still has some pull here, but what can she have them do that they aren't already?"

She sighed, resigned to the fact that even though all she wanted to do was act fast and strike down her enemies, all she could do was wait.

Or could she?

"Hanes wasn't working today, right?"

"VanBuren didn't mention whether he was or wasn't. He could have been at any one of the other stations, on shift."

"Text him." She reached behind him and pulled his phone out of his back pocket.

He tapped away as they walked out toward the road where they had parked. His phone pinged. "VanBuren said he is working at Station Three today. It's over on Thirty-Ninth and Russell." He looked at her. "His social media had him somewhere else at the time of the attack on his father, but it's easy to manipulate those time stamps."

"Let's go." She smiled. "And text Agent Hart and tell him to meet us there."

"Wait," he said, coming to a full stop as he neared his truck. "This isn't a good idea. First, they have to buzz us in, just like at headquarters. What do you think he is going to do if he sees us and he is the guy who is responsible for the bombs—and attack on his father?"

She scrunched her lips as her thoughts drifted through a variety of scenarios, some less bloody than others. "First, we don't know if he is responsible or not. I mean, I know he and his father have had some problems in the past, but why would he attack now? Out of the blue? And just because some chemicals are missing, chemicals he had access to and trained with… That wouldn't prove his guilt if you were standing in front of me and arguing this case."

"You know as well as I do that if this is the guy, he already wants you dead. If we back him into a corner and he gets wind that we have added him to our list of suspects, he will strike. Hard. Fast."

"And if he isn't, then we will be able to keep looking for who wants me dead." She could hear the exasperation in her tone, but it wasn't a frustration with him, just the entire situation. "I have been at risk since the moment I decided I wanted to work in the criminal justice sector. I regularly work with people who most would deem unstable. I knew that I would face danger every day with my job. Sure, this week has been a little hairier than most, but I'll make it through. I always do."

"Are you serious, Natalie?" He chuckled. "You know I can stand behind a dangerous job. I mean, look at me." He put his hand on his chest. "But that doesn't mean you put yourself in unnecessary danger just because you can. When you're in a foxhole, you don't stick your head up unless you want it to get shot off."

"Then I guess it's lucky we aren't in a foxhole." She smiled and got into the truck. He flopped in beside her and slammed the door behind him. "And, thankfully, I've got you at my side." She put her hand on his leg as she started the truck and slammed it into Reverse.

She was definitely being impetuous and playing with fire, but she was done being careful and hiding away. Besides, if things went as they had been, going to see this guy was just going to be another wild goose chase.

As she made her way out of downtown, Evan took out his gun and pulled back the slide.

"I'm telling you, I don't think anything bad is going to happen here." She shook her head at his extreme overreaction.

"You said you were ready for all the danger that comes with your job, but if you aren't a little bit nervous about what we are about to do, then you aren't as ready as you think." He slipped the gun back into the holster concealed in the waistband of his pants.

"If you are really worried about me," she said, pointing at her purse that was sitting between them on the truck's floorboard, "would you please put one in for me? I never carry with a chambered round."

He lifted his brow. "You have been carrying this whole time and you never told me?"

"The whole point of concealed carry is for it to be concealed." She winked at him. "Besides, you never asked."

"I should have known you wouldn't mess around," he said, reaching into her purse and unzipping the side compartment where she carried her Glock 42.

"I love that little gun," she said, looking at it fondly. "Fits into my running fanny pack perfectly and I can wear it under my robe without anyone being the wiser."

"Hey, you aren't supposed to carry in the courthouse." He laughed.

"Yeah, and I wouldn't if I thought all people were law-abiding citizens." She scoffed. "My bailiff can do a lot to keep me safe, but at the end of the day, my life rests in my hands."

"Not when I'm around."

She wasn't sure that she had ever heard anything more romantic. How had she gotten to have him in her life? He was such a complex mix—sweet and sexy, strong and capable, and best of all he was vulnerable and surprisingly open.

There had to be something about him that she didn't like…that she could use to keep from loving him, at least so soon. He supported her, wasn't even mildly sexist and he wanted the best for her. And yet, he was still the alpha male she had always been drawn to.

Yeah, she was so done for when it came to loving him.

He slipped her gun back into her purse after charging it for her. "Don't forget it's loaded. I can remind you when—"

There was the deafening roar of a diesel engine and the shattering of glass.

The world spun around her. Flipping and turning.

There was glass. Glass everywhere. The windshield crackled like when she was a child and had walked on too-thin ice. But under this ice, instead of the inky black of freezing cold water, there was the powdery explosion of snow and the whirling gray of the truck's hood flying up as they rolled.

The seat belt cut into her shoulder and across her stomach, holding her back. But there was something hard pressing against her chest and she looked down. Evan's hand was pressing into her sternum, like in this small action he could hold her back and keep her from being hurt.

Her head slammed against the airbag as it exploded from the side of the truck and the other exploded from the steering wheel. It hit her in the nose so hard that she could feel it start to bleed, but she couldn't tell if it was from inside or the outer bridge of her nose.

There was no pain.

Why was there no pain? There should have been pain by now—in her nose or maybe her shoulder.

She looked back down. Where had Evan's hand gone? Was he still touching her?

Yes. There was his hand. She closed her eyes and looked over at where her hand was also on him and sandwiched between him and his airbag.

They had both tried to protect each other.

The truck skidded to a stop, jerking her hard against the side. It took her a minute to get her bearings. Somehow, the truck had come to rest back on its tires, or what was left of them, but it listed to the right and the air was filled with the acrid scent of antifreeze and smoke.

"What...what happened?" she asked, though

not to anyone more than herself. "Evan. Evan, are you okay?"

His face was pressed into the steadily deflating airbag and his eyes were closed. If she hadn't known better, she would have thought he was just catching a catnap.

"Evan?" she said again, her voice strangled.

He didn't move.

There were the sounds of voices around her, men yelling something she couldn't quite understand. All she could think about was Evan and the thin bead of blood that was starting to flow from somewhere above his eye and in his hairline. If his blood was flowing, that had to mean he was still alive. Right?

She pressed her hand harder against his chest and touched his hand resting on hers with her other. Focusing, she could feel a heartbeat but she wasn't completely sure if it was his or if it was hers. The fabric of his shirt was thick, the kind that pilled with too many washes.

"It's going to be okay, honey. I'm going to get you out of this." She didn't think he could hear her, but it didn't matter; she had to say the words.

Here he had been promising her that he would do everything in his power to protect her, and life had come out of nowhere and stripped them both of the one thing they wanted—to stay safe.

If she didn't do something quickly, it would take his life, too.

She moved to undo her seat belt, but her fingers fumbled with the latch. It was like her fingertips were heavy, weighted down with the adrenaline and the fear that was coursing through her. As she moved to release the belt, she looked up at a flurry of motion outside his window. A firetruck was careening toward them.

It was coming too fast.

It was coming straight at them.

It was going to hit Evan's side.

She pressed the gas pedal down as hard as she could, not sure if the truck was even running or not. The engine sputtered but the truck lurched forward a few feet.

The firetruck struck, hitting the bed of the mangled truck and spinning them around like a top. Her head hit the deflating airbag to her left, but she didn't feel pain. Only shock.

A firetruck. Hit. Them. They had been attacked using a machine usually driven by heroes, men and women who had been called down to save them. This driver, this plastic hero, wanted them *dead*.

She fumbled for her purse, thinking about the gun inside, but her seat belt held her back.

Evan had a gun, but it was too far away and out of reach.

She took a breath, trying to click her brain into gear. She had to move. Sitting still only meant death.

There had to be a way.

She pressed on the gas pedal with her left foot, not caring where the truck edged to as long as they moved. The engine sputtered again, clicking as smoke started to fill the cab. With her right foot she swept the floor until she found her purse. She wiggled the toe of her boot into the purse's strap and lifted it until she could grab hold. Reaching in, she pulled out her gun, stripping it from its holster.

The truck shuddered and died. They were sitting ducks.

She lifted her gun to a low, ready position. Evan's head was pressed against the side of the door, and the blood was flowing steady and hard from the gash that had reopened over his eye. Blood streamed down the back of his neck and was staining the cloth headrest behind him.

As she stared at him, she could smell his clean, fresh cologne mix through the acrid smoke.

Her side window was gone even though she didn't remember hearing it break. As she realized it, she felt the shards and crumbles of glass that were piercing into her hands as she held the gun low in her lap.

Screams. There were the sounds of screams.

She looked out the broken windshield. The firetruck was sitting askew on the road in front of her, head-on. The driver's seat was empty and the door was open. So was the passenger's door.

Had there been two people in the firetruck?

What was going on?

A woman appeared a few feet from her window. Her raven hair glistened like a freshly sharpened blade in the wintry sun.

It was the renter, the woman whom they had spoken to. The woman who had been staying at Ms. Rencher's old place. But why…why would she be here?

"I bet you thought you wouldn't see me again." The woman sent her a wicked smile, giving her the appearance of a crazed beast.

"What in the hell are you doing?" Natalie asked.

"I'm getting you out of our way, Ms. Goody Two-shoes."

There was something hilariously outdated in the woman's jibe and strangely, Natalie felt the urge to laugh at the craziness of it all. Had she hit the hysteria level of shock?

"Getting me out of the way of what?" she

asked, careful to slide her gun under the edge of her shirt and out of sight of the approaching woman.

There was the crunch of glass on pavement and she turned to see Sven Hanes standing outside Evan's door. He reached down and tried to open the door, but it was jammed. Thankfully, the window on that side was still intact, though she couldn't imagine how.

"Kill her, Becky." Sven pointed at his neck.

"Why? Why do you want me dead?" she asked again, struggling to make sense of everything.

"Shut up. Just shut up." Becky snarled at him. "Your screwups have already gotten us into enough trouble."

So not all was well in love land.

"Becky, it's not too late," she started, hoping she could have a chance at talking the woman down.

The woman chuckled as she pulled a syringe out of her pocket.

"You don't have to do this. I'm a judge and if you stop right now, I can make sure that you are treated fairly when you are arrested. Just don't do anything you're going to regret." Natalie put the palm of her free hand up, surrendering. The last thing she wanted to do was to draw down on this woman and pull the trigger.

"I don't know how you got yourself into this situation with Sven, but it's not too late to do the right thing. Make the right choice. I know how hard this kind of thing can be and how hard it can be to get out of it."

"I know exactly who you are. And if you would have just gone along with my sister, we wouldn't have to be in this mess." The woman glowered down at her. "You are the one who screwed everything up. You put everyone at risk."

"Your sister?" she asked, now totally confused.

"The district attorney. She asked you to play along. All you had to do was say yes. Steve and Sven had a great thing going and they made a lot of money working with the DA to get things done. But you had to eff it all up. This…all of this, is on your head."

She had known the district attorney had made a gesture to see how amenable Natalie was to being bought, but she had no idea that it was because she already had a thing going on with Judge Hanes—Natalie's friend. The judge who had brought her into the fold. The judge who had trained her. Who had basically gotten her a seat on the bench.

He had set her up. He had used her to grow his crooked dealings.

But why? Why had his son and Becky tried to hurt him?

She wanted to tell the woman she sounded crazy and that there were a million other ways around the situation that they were in, but Becky wasn't going to listen. She was frenzied…backed into the corner like a snarling dog and now it was fight or die.

"Whatever it is that you think I screwed up, don't you think we could *fix* it?" she asked, playing her deadly game.

"Don't you think it's a little too late for that?" Becky sneered. "*Our* plan is going along just fine. All that's left is for you and your crappy little guard over there to get a dirt bath."

A dirt bath?

"You haven't done this kind of thing before, have you?" she asked.

Out of the corner of her eye, she saw Sven walking around the front end of the truck. He stopped as a bystander started to come over to help. Sven put up his hands, but she was forced to look back at the most immediate threat— Becky.

Becky moved toward her, the needle mostly concealed by her hand; only the tip was sticking out.

Natalie jerked, putting up her left arm in self-defense. The woman laughed, the sound sour and angry as their arms connected. Becky grabbed her hand and pressed her arm down and into the broken glass that was smattered on the windowsill. The glass cut into her arm and she gripped the gun in her hand, hard.

All she had to do was pull the trigger.

Becky lunged, the needle moved toward her and she watched it happen in slow motion as something in her lizard brain clicked into place. Kill or be killed.

She was a fighter. But if she pulled the trigger, she would have to spend every night after this thinking about all the other things she could have done to get out of this situation. There had to be another way.

There was a loud boom, and the air around her reverberated with the gunshot.

Had she pulled the trigger? She looked down, confused as she pulled the gun from beneath the edge of her bloodied shirt. Her finger wasn't even on the trigger.

Evan said something, but she only heard the muffle of his voice and couldn't make out the edges of his words in the ringing deafness left by the gunshot.

His hand moved off her chest and he took hold of her shoulder. In his right hand, the trigger still pinned, was the gun. He shook her as he looked at her. His mouth moved and she could tell he was asking her if she was okay, but she didn't know how to respond.

She moved her hand up to her neck, feeling for Becky's needle. There was nothing. Nothing protruding out of her neck, only the slivers and grit of exploded glass.

Her gaze moved over toward the window. Becky was no longer standing beside her, but her hand was still on her arm, pressing it into the glass. She lifted up her arm and pulled it out of the woman's limp grip.

Dead or alive, she didn't care.

Sven turned, he reached down like he was going for a gun, but before he could clear and pull, she already had her gun pointed at him. When had she drawn?

She moved her finger to the trigger, pressing down the safety and easing it back.

"No!" Evan yelled.

Releasing her grip, the trigger slipped forward and back on safe.

The bystander who had been coming toward them grabbed Sven from behind, throwing him to the ground.

As the man moved, she saw a flash of a badge and a set of silver handcuffs come out from behind the stranger's back. He slapped them on Sven's wrists.

"Are you okay?" Evan's hand tightened on her shoulder.

She nodded.

"Give me your gun," Evan said, extending his hand.

As she moved to hand it over, the gun shook violently. If she'd been forced to pull the trigger, she had no idea what she would have hit, but she doubted it would have been Becky.

He took the gun and slipped the mag out and emptied the chamber. The round dropped into his lap and he picked it up and put it back into the mag. "I will give this back to you later. I'm sure that the police will want to hear all about what has happened here."

"Thank you…" she said, suddenly aware of everything that was going to come next—the hospital, the police, the lawyers, the courtrooms. They would be cleared, without a doubt, given everything that had happened and the scene Becky and Sven had created in their attempt to kill them.

Evan smirked, his lip was starting to grow puffy and there was a split on the bottom. "No need to thank me, ma'am."

"I'll take it that you are okay?" she asked, staring at the cut that was starting to bleed on his lip.

He put his fingers up to the reopened cut on his forehead. "I think I'll be fine with a fresh dab of skin glue, a couple Tylenol and an ice pack."

She pointed down at his legs where the door had been crushed inward. "Your legs?"

"Good." He wiggled his feet and lifted his knees. He glanced out at the smoking firetruck and the police cars that were skidding to a halt on the icy intersection around them. "As for the city, I think we've done a number on it."

She laughed, but then felt ridiculous for doing so.

He let go of her shoulder and took her shaking hand in his. Lifting their hands, he gave her knuckles a kiss. "We are going to be okay. We're in this together."

They sat there for a long moment, collecting themselves.

A police officer rushed over to the truck and squatted down beside Becky and she assumed he was taking her pulse. He stood back up and peered in at them, assessing the situation. "You okay?"

They both nodded.

"Just don't move. We will be with you in just a minute." The officer turned his head toward his handset and started talking to the dispatcher on the other end of the radio.

Evan squeezed her hand. "Babe?"

"Yeah?" she asked, looking over at him in all of his bruised glory.

"I need you to promise me something." He smiled, but winced as the split in his lip opened and his smile faded from view.

"Hmm?" She looked out at the melee of action around them.

"When we get through this… I want us to be together. Like you move into my place. Okay?"

She slowly turned her head to face him. "What?"

"I want to take you out, into public, for a real date. Spaghetti, wine, dancing…the whole thing. And if that doesn't sell you, I must add that I can dance."

"Spaghetti and a dance? Is that the best you've got?" she teased.

"Hey, don't bash spaghetti. What has it ever done to you?"

"Okay, I'll move in and you can take me to have spaghetti and go dancing…but only if you promise me something in return."

"Whatever you want." He squeezed.

She smiled at him. "I want to keep you, forever. I clearly can't go anywhere without my protector—and the man I love." She leaned over and their lips met.

"I love you, too, baby." He nodded. "And clearly, I can't go anywhere without mine. We are in this together."

Epilogue

Three months later everything had started to quiet back down in the little city. The cuts, bruises and her sprained ankle had healed and she was finally starting to feel almost back to her normal self once again. It was odd, but the hardest part of going through a gauntlet of death threats was not the initial action, but the echoing silence that came afterward.

She was always looking over her shoulder, wondering who would be following her and ready to draw a gun. And when having to drive somewhere, she never got in before hitting her key fob at least twice and actively looking under her car.

Yes, Sven and Becky had been caught, and the direct threats to her life had ended, but the fear they had created within her had failed to subside. Maybe one day she could get into a car without being afraid it would blow up, but here was hoping.

Evan opened the restaurant door for her and motioned for her to step inside. She glanced over her shoulder one more time.

"Don't worry, honey," he said, but not before she saw him do the exact same thing.

He would never admit that he was still on high alert; he would only tell her that this was his normal level of awareness, nothing more. She found it draining, but it also brought her a strange sense of comfort.

The hostess at the Italian restaurant greeted them and led them to a table in the back. "Will this do?" she asked.

"Yep, thank you very much." Evan pulled back Natalie's chair and helped her get settled and then he took his seat with his back to the wall.

The hostess retreated, leaving them to listen to the little string band that was playing "My Way." It was strangely sad but it fit the day. Evan reached over and took her hand in his. "I'm glad we finally found time to have a date, honey. I'm just sorry that you and I have to do it after such a ridiculous week."

It was just the break she needed after the flurry of cases she had been allotted after Hanes had been dismissed as a judge, pending investigation of any deals he'd made in the past. Even if he hadn't been fired, he would never have been able to come back. The nerve agent had done significant cognitive and pulmonary damage.

"Steve was moved back into the ICU today. Apparently, he fell and hit his head on his hospital bed." She ran her thumb over the back of Evan's hand.

"I know you're struggling with this, honey, but you couldn't have changed a damned thing. Steve made some bad choices. His son made bad choices."

"I know you and I talked about the fates, but can you imagine how different everything would have turned out if Steve's wife hadn't been killed by a drunk driver?" She paused. "Sven wouldn't have had half the problems he had. He wouldn't have forced his father into unethical positions to save him. One choice, a seemingly independent decision made by a stranger…one who I will never know, ended up almost costing you and me our lives, as well."

"You know these things… It's life. It is chaos. Plain and simple." He squeezed her hand.

"I'm just glad I was able to help set things right for all the people whose cases and lives were screwed up because of Judge Hanes, his son, the crooked district attorney and her sister." She couldn't stand the thought of how one simple conversation with the district attorney could have sent her on a completely different trajectory.

"Do you think Sven and Becky knew what they were doing when they used the Rockwood plates in their bombs?"

Evan shook his head. "According to his lawyers, Sven didn't know about any ties my family has to the group. But I still have a feeling that there is something more there. Regardless, I think Sven is going to play the insanity card as his defense in court."

"I have a feeling a judge will see right through that. Sven is going to have a nice long stay in a federal prison." She couldn't help the smile that flit across her lips. "And so far, the court of appeals has overturned several of Judge Hanes's rulings and many innocent people have been released from prison."

"I can only imagine how many guilty people are walking free because of them," Evan said, shaking his head in disgust.

The waiter came over and took their orders—two heaping plates of spaghetti and a bottle of Chianti.

Evan smiled as the man walked away. "Regardless of what has brought us together, I want you to know that I'm grateful. You are all I can think of, morning, noon and night. You are always on my mind. I don't think that will ever change. It's like, in meeting you, I found my soul's other half."

She put her hand on her heart like it could control her swoon. "Honey, I love you, too."

The band started their next Sinatra song, "I've Got the World on a String."

She smiled as he stood up and extended his hand. She slipped her fingers in his.

"Can I have this dance?" he asked, straightening his suit jacket as she stood.

Her dress pulled around her legs, forcing her to take small steps to the center of the room. It felt like all eyes were on them. He led her in a graceful dance, and his subtle control made her feel more beautiful than she had in her entire life. She felt like a swan, gliding around the room like her feet didn't even touch the floor.

"I had no idea you were such a good dancer," she said, whispering into his ear and then returning to gaze into his beautiful green eyes.

They were alight with joy as he looked at her. "My mother made sure I took dance lessons as a kid. I hate to admit it, but I was an All-State Ballroom dancer when I was a senior in high school."

"Your mother was a smart woman. This is one timeless and elegant way to make a woman fall madly in love."

His smile widened. "I thought you were already madly in love with me."

"I love you more every day." She gave him a light kiss to the cheek as he pulled her into his arms before he spun her out of his grip.

She giggled as he moved her. It felt oddly invigorating to be at the mercy of such an incredible dancer. She was dancing out of her league, but she didn't care.

He pulled her back against him, hard. Apparently, he was having a good time, as well.

"I can think of nothing better than being in your arms like this," she said, nearly breathless. "I know we've waited a long time to have a night completely for us, but this is beyond any expectations."

"Most of the time, I would agree with you," he said, leading her around the dance floor. "Yet, there is something I can think of that would make our long-awaited date just that much better."

She giggled. "What is that?"

"If you would wear this," he said, dropping to his knee and opening up a box she hadn't seen him take out of his pocket.

At the heart of the box was a princess-cut diamond and set beside it was a set of sapphires. It was beautiful.

"Baby, yes…" she said, putting her hands over her mouth and then extending her left one.

He slipped the ring on her finger and stood up. Taking her lips with his, they needed no words. In that moment she had everything she would ever need or want and she could share it all with a man who was her equal.

No matter what the future held, or the chaos they would face, they would face it standing beside one another. They would be one another's shields from the ravages of the world—and they would do it all empowered by the strength and ferocity of their love.

* * * * *

Get 4 FREE REWARDS!

We'll send you 2 FREE Books plus 2 FREE Mystery Gifts.

Harlequin Presents books feature the glamorous lives of royals and billionaires in a world of exotic locations, where passion knows no bounds.

FREE Value Over $20

Get 4 FREE REWARDS!

We'll send you 2 FREE Books plus 2 FREE Mystery Gifts.

FREE Value Over **$20**

Both the **Romance** and **Suspense** collections feature compelling novels written by many of today's bestselling authors.